THE VAMPIRE'S TOUCH

A midlife paranormal mystery thriller

MEMORY GUILD BOOK 9

WARD PARKER

Mad Mangrove Media

CONTENTS

CHAPTER 1

MR. JUBBLES' TROUBLES

He was stealing a snack in the middle of the night and became a snack himself.

Mr. Jubbles lay in a heap inside the pantry, the bulk bin of cocktail peanuts spilled on the floor beside him, as if he had tumbled from the same container.

I had entered the pantry to retrieve these nuts for Wine Hour. None of the staff had been in it all day, and Mr. Jubbles couldn't have been without being caught. So, the poor man had lain here since last night.

Poor Mr. Jubbles. I had been surprised when he booked this stay with us after Sophie scolded him for stealing towels the last time he was here. And after he witnessed an attack by monsters called anthropophagi—that he fortunately forgot about, thanks to being blackout drunk.

But why did he break into the pantry? I keep a tray of cookies and a bowl of fruit on a table in the foyer for guests to snack on. Small discreet placards outside the kitchen and the pantry announce these spaces are for employees only. Occasionally, a guest has been known to raid the refrigerator overnight in search of leftover breakfast goodies or canapés from the Wine Hour that I didn't devour myself.

It was unheard of for a guest to raid the pantry—basically a large supply closet—because it was supposed to be locked. Sophie, who had handled last night's Wine Hour for me, must have forgotten to lock it.

The instant I saw Mr. Jubbles, I felt his frigid neck for a pulse, although it was unlikely that he was still alive. It was difficult to get to his neck with his droopy jowls in the way. A small amount of blood was smeared beside his mouth—possibly from a hemorrhage or a cut from falling. He was also unnaturally pale, but being dead can do that to you.

No pulse. Sadly, he was deceased. My guess that it was a cardiac incident was quickly dashed when I saw the twin puncture wounds on his neck.

Uh-oh. It was bad enough for a guest to die in our inn. We've had too many do so. But to be drained by a vampire? That could put us out of business for sure. The inn's reputation for being haunted was, in fact, a draw for some guests. But they would not appreciate the possibility of being preyed upon by a blood-sucking fiend.

Did Roderick do this? My resident vampire, who slept in a crawlspace behind the refrigerator, knew better than to mess with guests. Nevertheless, he was my prime suspect right now. Sunset would arrive soon, and I would question him as soon as he emerged from his lair.

I'd almost forgotten about Wine Hour. How could I host a gathering of guests sipping Chardonnay while Mr. Jubbles lay here just around the corner?

And how could I distract them while an EMS crew carted

the body away? Well, Mr. Jubbles has been here since last night, an extra hour or so won't hurt him.

"Oh, no!" Cory blurted out behind me, causing me to jump in surprise. "Is that Mr. Jubbles?" He ran his hands nervously through his straight sandy-blond hair.

"Yep."

"Heart attack?"

"Vampire attack."

"Oh no."

"Oh yes. Let's just leave him in here until Wine Hour is over."

"We can't do that. Are you crazy? We need to take care of him immediately."

"He's dead. He's in no hurry."

"Knock it off with the macabre humor, Darla. I'm calling nine-one-one."

"It's more complicated than that. Technically, this is a murder. He was drained by the vampire. But we can't talk about vampires to the authorities. We can play dumb, and let the EMTs and medical examiner come up with a preposterous explanation of how he died without involving the supernatural. But it would probably be criminal not to say we know a vampire did it. A vampire who's not supposed to exist."

"You should call Detective Samson," Cory said. "He's the only cop we can trust."

"Yeah. This is all going to look terrible for our guests."

"We have no choice. It's too bad we can't contact the Vampire Guild, but they're all stark raving mad from the evil magic that infected them."

"I'll call Diego."

A member of both the Memory Guild and the Clan of the

Eternal Night, he was one of the very few vampires in San Marcos who wasn't infected.

"Do you think Roderick did this?" he asked.

"I hope not," I said. "He knows better, but preying on guests got him in trouble back when he owned the place in the late eighteen hundreds. I'll ask him as soon as he wakes up. In the meantime, please help me set up for Wine Hour, and I'll call Samson."

I handed him three bottles of red and told him which bottles of white to retrieve from the wine fridge. After he left the pantry, I called Samson.

"Are you busy?"

"Actually, I'm about to go home for the day," he replied.

"Um, sorry to delay you, but we need help."

"Don't tell me you've had another murder at the inn."

"Will you stop it? You make it sound like lots of our guests have been killed."

"You've had your fair share."

"Well, we've added one more to the list."

"You've got to be kidding me."

"Unfortunately, not. A Mr. Jubbles from Yeehaw Junction was killed by a vampire."

"A human killed by a supernatural. That's a big problem."

"Tell me about it. I'm assuming it was a vampire turned feral by the evil spell."

Even though the Fae have halted their assault on us, the spell they released is still making the vampires try to turn every living creature into a vampire.

"Weren't you working on fixing that spell?"

"You know it's beyond my abilities. I need an ally with serious magic. And Arch Mage Bob tried unsuccessfully several times. The Faerie Queene said she can't reverse the spell either."

"The vampires won't stop until the entire city is turned."

"Well, I hope it doesn't get *that* bad. But anyway, can you come by after Wine Hour is over? I don't want to disturb my guests."

"If we enter a vampire apocalypse, you won't have any more guests coming to San Marcos."

"Don't be so melodramatic. I'll see you at six."

Only seven guests showed up for tonight's event. Mr. Jubbles, had he not met an unfortunate end, would have been the eighth and would have consumed the lion's share of the wine. There were no cocktail peanuts to serve because they were on the floor of the pantry beside and beneath Mr. Jubbles. I served cheese and crackers, plus mini egg rolls, instead.

A loud crash came from the direction of the kitchen. A couple of guests looked up before returning to their conversations.

A door rattled and opened. The pantry door.

Cory was in the foyer with our guests, so it wasn't him. I was pretty sure Sophie was up in her room.

Slow, heavy steps came down the hallway. A muffled sob.

I slipped away down the hall, stopping at the intersection with the hall that passed the kitchen and pantry and led to the dining and living rooms.

Mr. Jubbles was staggering toward me.

Holy moly! The vampire who killed him had also turned him. When I found Mr. Jubbles in the pantry, he hadn't been dead— only undead. The blood by his mouth must have belonged to the vampire who undid Mr. Jubbles' mortality.

Mr. Jubbles, pale as a corpse, disheveled and confused, stared at me hungrily. He sniffed, and his eyes widened as he caught the scent of my guests in the foyer.

"Hungry," he said to me, as if he expected the innkeeper to

cater to his needs and fetch him someone to bite. Sorry, this isn't a five-star hotel.

"No," I said. "Go home."

Not that I expected him to drive back to Yeehaw Junction in his state of mind, but I didn't know what else to say.

He staggered toward me. I retrieved the crucifix from my pocket, that I'd been carrying ever since the vampires became infected, and thrust it toward him.

He stopped and blinked stupidly at the tiny silver cross. These don't work on experienced, more powerful vampires, but it was working on this newbie.

Freshly turned vampires need extensive care from their makers to help them adjust to their new existence. The feral vampire who made him obviously wasn't bothering to fulfill his or her responsibilities. The only bright side to this was the evidence showing that while vampires infected by the spell can pass it on to other vampires, they don't infect the next-generation vampires they create.

Look at me: always finding a bright spot in the darkness.

"Roderick, help me," I called in a voice too low for the guests to hear, but easily audible to a vampire.

The young couple from Savannah in room 303 wandered down the hall toward us. I stepped toward them, trying to block their view of Mr. Jubbles.

"And where are you guys planning to dine tonight?" I asked with a strained smile. "I have several excellent places to recommend."

"Hungry!" Mr. Jubbles said behind me.

"We're not going wherever he's going," the wife said to her husband.

"Don't mind Mr. Jubbles," I said. "He's having a little episode. Do you mind giving him some privacy?"

I gave a nod in the foyer's direction, and the couple got my hint. They turned and strolled back to the festivities, which were winding down.

"I crave blood! Must feed!"

I shushed Mr. Jubbles and tried to herd him back toward the pantry using the crucifix. He was reluctant. I guess the scent of living humans was too much for him. His stomach growled. When that happens to us humans, it sounds funny. When it's a vampire's stomach, it's horrifying.

"What is going on here? Why did you awaken me at the crack of dusk?" Roderick asked, exiting the kitchen. He frowned when he saw Mr. Jubbles. "Who is this uncouth vampire?"

"A guest who was just turned. You didn't do it, did you?"

"Of course not. I would never feed on a guest." He rubbed the sleep from his eyes. "Not anymore, at least."

"Can you help me? I don't know what to do with him. He's a danger to all the humans here."

"I'm not much given to babysitting new vampires."

"Hungry!" Mr. Jubbles whined.

"Can you take him outside and find a rat or something?"

I knew Roderick was not above feeding on animals. This was because he was inept at mesmerizing human prey, so he wisely avoided them.

"Come with me, child, and I'll help you feed," he said to Mr. Jubbles, grabbing him by the upper arm and ushering him toward the back door.

The main door chimed as Detective Michael Samson walked in.

"Where is the victim?"

"He just stepped out to get a bite to eat."

"I thought he was deceased."

7

"Turns out he's undead. That's good, right? No paperwork for you to file. One less murder occurring in my inn."

Samson shook his head. "Well, technically, it's a murder since the victim was killed. But if he's up and about, doing stuff, and contributing to our tourist economy, then we can't really record him as a homicide victim. In my eyes, it's not good to have another vampire hunting in our city, though."

"They weren't much of a problem until now."

"And now, they're a massive problem. They're going to upset the balance that has existed since the dawn of civilization—supernaturals living undetected among humans. There's going to be hysteria and conspiracy theories. Neighbors are going to stake one another because of something they read on social media, while the vampires will keep creating more of their kind."

"It's not my job to solve this problem."

"You're a goddess, aren't you? Who better than you to solve it?"

I sighed. Being a goddess was overrated. Especially when you're merely the human incarnation of an ancient Celtic earth-mother goddess. I stopped an attack of feral vampires once, but I don't have enough power to heal them of this spell.

"Where was the victim attacked and turned?" Samson asked.

"In here." I opened the door to the pantry and pointed to the floor covered in cocktail peanuts. "Oh, what's this?"

A bracelet lay on the floor. I hadn't seen it before because it must have been beneath Mr. Jubbles. It was a woman's antique bangle made of gold, shaped like a snake. Did it fall off the wrist of the vampire who turned Mr. Jubbles?

I bent to reach for it when Samson stopped me.

"I better have it dusted for fingerprints. It's doubtful we'll get a match, but you never know."

8

He tore off a piece of aluminum foil from a roll on a nearby shelf and carefully wrapped the bracelet in it.

"If this vampire poses an ongoing threat to our citizens, then we'll have to track her down and stake her because the Clan of the Eternal Night can't enforce their rules right now. What are you going to do with your guest?"

"Check him out and tell him to return to Yeehaw Junction as soon as he's okay to drive. Unless it turns out he's infected by the spell and can't think logically."

"I'm afraid that will be your problem." He gave me a smile and a wink and quickly disappeared.

I cleaned up the remnants from Wine Hour, then set upon sweeping up the spilled peanuts from the pantry before they attracted pests. It made me wonder if Mr. Jubbles was having any luck catching rats.

A stinging stench drifted in from the direction of the alley. The bell for the delivery entrance rang.

Uh-oh.

I passed through the utility room and reached the back door to the alley. I opened it a crack.

Roderick stood outside with a forlorn expression on his face. He reeked of the stench I now recognized as skunk spray.

"I didn't think there were any skunks left in San Marcos," I said.

"Mr. Jubbles found one. I was trying to show him how to hunt rats and possums, but the idiot attacked the skunk. You know, of course, that vampires have super-powered senses. Can you imagine how much olfactory suffering I'm enduring right now?"

"Both of you were sprayed?"

"Mostly him, but I was hit, too."

"Hungry," Mr. Jubbles said from farther down the alley.

"You shut up," Roderick told him. "That skunk should be more than enough to sustain you until tomorrow evening."

"I guess newly turned vampires have enormous appetites," I said.

"It's not my responsibility."

"Look, if you found a helpless infant abandoned in the street, you wouldn't just leave it there."

"No, I would give it to the authorities."

"There aren't any authorities at the moment for vampires."

"Are you implying that I must care for this idiot?"

"A newly turned vampire is virtually helpless without support and training. Do you want him to hang around the inn forever?"

"Of course not!"

"Then teach him how to survive on his own so he can return to his hometown."

"I have no patience for teaching morons."

"You owe it to your kind."

Roderick sputtered. He couldn't think of a rejoinder.

"And don't come into this building until you've cleaned off that smell," I said, closing the door.

I needed some clear-headed vampire advice, so I called Diego.

"You did the right thing in asking Roderick to care for the child," he said.

I still couldn't get over Roderick and Diego calling the septuagenarian Mr. Jubbles a child, but between the two vampires, they were hundreds of years older.

"I don't feel it's safe for me or my guests to let Mr. Jubbles stay in his room during his transition period."

"Yes, you are correct. This child should stay with Roderick."

"In his tiny crawlspace? Oh, Roderick won't like that one bit."

"It's the only prudent thing to do. Also, you must keep an eye out for the child's maker, who might show up again."

I shivered at the thought. I still didn't know how the vampire got inside the inn at night, but that's what vampires are good at.

Describing the bracelet I found in the pantry, I asked Diego if it sounded familiar to him.

"No, but it is intriguing. I would like to find out who is preying on humans so shamelessly, flaunting the most funda-mental rule of vampires in human society. Too bad I can't ask around to my fellow vampires since they're all insane now. We must stop this vampire from striking again and putting us all in danger."

And putting my inn's reputation in danger.

CHAPTER 2

DIVINE LONGING

Cory and I sat at our tiny dining table beside the tiny kitchen in our tiny cottage, waiting for Sophie to arrive. We didn't use the inn's main dining room, where breakfast and afternoon tea were served, because we wanted privacy and family intimacy. Instead, we got a twenty-five-year-old daughter behaving like a teenager.

I texted, then called her. No answer.

"I'm going up to check on her," I said, pushing my chair back.

Before I knocked on her third-floor door, I smelled the incense leaking out. I recognized it as a noxious mixture of dried herbs and roots the Fae often used in their magic. Baldric, the Chief of the Guild of Fae and Wee People, introduced it to her when he taught her the Fae magic she used to supplement her human elemental magic.

"Sophie, we're waiting for you for dinner," I said to the door. "You can practice your magic after dessert."

She didn't answer.

I knocked. "Sophie, are you okay?"

She moaned. I wasn't sure if it was from pain or pleasure.

She'd been talking about having a crush on Haarg, the Fae God of War. I guess I should be lucky my daughter was not in love with a criminal, but why couldn't he be a human? Specifically, a doctor or lawyer? Why a Fae god—and one of war, of all things?

Yeah, I know it sounds hypocritical for me, now that I've been thrust into the role of goddess incarnate. It's no fun, I tell you. I didn't want my daughter to be caught up in the schemes of immortals. If you know your mythology, humans who are romanced by gods and demigods rarely come to good ends.

Was it too much to prefer she fell in love with a cute hedge-fund manager?

She moaned again. This one sounded painful. I was no longer concerned she had snuck a boy—or god—into her room. Now, I was worried about her safety.

I used the passkey to open the door, which she really hates for me to do.

The room was dimly lit with ancient-looking oil lamps. A brass dish filled with the noxious incense burned on the nightstand.

Sophie lay fully clothed atop her bed, bathed in sweat, writhing in what appeared to be agony.

"Sweetie? Are you okay?"

I approached the bed and put my hand on her forehead. It was burning with fever. Her eyelids twitched from vivid dreams.

Was she possessed by an entity? Haarg, perhaps?

I've never met him myself, but could you really trust a god of war?

It was time to put the Goddess's healing powers to work. I closed my eyes and focused on my interior, drawing out the power of the Goddess Danu. A warm tingling began in my solar plexus and spread within me. I placed my palms on either side of Sophie's head and felt the warmth flow through my arms and hands into her.

The warmth of love to fight the heat of fever.

A song took me over—an ancient one that I didn't recognize. Words in ancient Gaelic that I did not understand poured from my mouth in tune with the music in my head.

The energy in Sophie shifted. Her skin cooled quickly and dramatically, while her breathing slowed.

As if in reaction to her fever subsiding, the warmth inside me faded, as well. The song in my head and heart ceased. Now, I was Darla again, ministering to my daughter as I had hundreds of times when she was young.

Briefly, ever so briefly, I felt the mother-daughter bond that is so strong, complicated, and unlike any other.

"Mom! What are you doing in here?"

Talk about killing the mood.

"You were feverish and in distress," I said. "I was concerned."

"I was communicating with Haarg. Ever since I came to his attention, through Baldric's magic, we've been becoming closer. I'm trying to find the best ways to use my own magic to communicate with him."

"What's so special about him? Why are you attracted to a god of war—of killing and destruction?"

"Because he's hot." She had a dreamy look in her eyes.

"Yeah, that's something."

"And he's so charismatic. Just because he's a war god doesn't make him evil. War has always been a part of intelligent species. Haarg turns the brutality of war into the art of war."

"I see."

"And he's so strong and intense."

"Of course. But wouldn't you rather be involved with a human who can take you out for dinner and a movie?"

"Haarg can take me to the heavens and beyond."

"Yeah, there's that."

"Ancient gods normally take on the forms of humans or animals to visit earth. Haarg promised to see me in human form soon. I hope he's as hot as his spiritual entity."

"Is he going to create a human or possess one who already exists?"

She looked stumped. "He didn't say. I'm not sure how it works."

"Because if he possesses an existing human, you'll have all of that guy's baggage to deal with."

"I hadn't thought of that."

"Just a warning to the wise."

"You're not supportive of our relationship," Sophie said.

"I want you to be happy. Based on my personal experience, dealing with a deity isn't fun and games. And something tells me the Fae God of War might not get along with the Celtic earth-mother goddess."

"Husbands and mothers-in-law often have tensions. They get over it."

"*Husband?*"

"Okay, maybe I'm getting ahead of myself."

"Let's talk about this later. Cory and I and dinner are waiting for you."

"Mortal existence is so boring."

ON MY WAY BACK TO THE COTTAGE, I HEARD VOICES IN THE kitchen. The lights were off, but the two individuals in the room didn't need lights to see. That was one advantage of being a vampire and a gargoyle.

I snapped on the lights. Roderick blinked at me, and Archibald gave me a sardonic stare.

"Really?" said the stone imp. "Rather rude, I shall say."

He was perched on the subway tile above the kitchen counter where a chessboard was set up. Roderick sat on a stool facing him.

"Didn't I tell you guys to stay out of sight before midnight, so guests won't see you?"

"We were in the dark," Roderick said. "Emphasis on 'were.'"

"A guest looking for snacks could have turned on the light," I countered. "Like poor Mr. Jubbles when he was human. How is he doing, by the way?"

Roderick inclined his head toward the door to the crawl-space. It was normally covered by the smaller of two refrigerators, which he rolled out of the way when he went in or out.

"He's in there having one of his regular crying fits. So melodramatic."

"I'm sure your transition when you were turned was difficult, too," I said.

"We were much more stoic in that day and age. The American version of the English stiff upper lip."

"Oh, please," sneered Archibald, whose lip was very literally stiff most of the time.

"Is Mr. Jubbles making any progress?" I asked.

"Minor. He has finally learned to catch small creatures that don't spray you with noxious substances."

"The sooner he can get by on his own, the better for both of us. His reservations have run their course, and I need to get his belongings out of his room so I can book it to new guests. We're already short two additional rooms while they're being deep

16

cleaned after the faeries finally moved out. Wilference and the Queene left disgusting messes behind."

"The Fae fancy themselves as superior to humans, but not in all ways," Archibald said.

"Agreed. Now, Roderick, have you sensed Mr. Jubbles' maker lurking around the inn?"

"I have indeed sensed a vampire lurking. I cannot tell if she is his maker. She hasn't come across as a threat. Yet. Unfortunately, one got past my defenses and attacked Mr. Jubbles in my home."

"Not difficult to do," Archibald muttered.

"I am certain she did so while I was out hunting," Roderick said.

"It's a female?" I asked.

"Yes."

"If the bracelet belonged to her, she might want it back. I'll have Samson return it to avoid trouble."

"If she's not infected, she might return looking for the bracelet or to administer the duties to her child she has neglected," Roderick said. "If she's under the influence of the spell, she'll come here only to drain and turn humans."

I shuddered. "We're lucky Mr. Jubbles is unmarried, and we won't have to deal with his spouse freaking out that her husband became a vampire in my inn. I can't afford to have any more guests turned."

"*My* inn," Roderick corrected.

"We've been through this a million times already. You lost the inn to foreclosure over a century ago. I purchased it fair and square."

"What if Mr. Jubbles has other family or friends who discover he was turned here?" Archibald asked.

"I'm hoping to get him back to Yeehaw Junction in a rational state of mind as soon as possible. I assume he would conceal his vampirism from friends and family. If they find out, hopefully he won't tell them where he was turned."

"Is there really a place called Yeehaw Junction?" Archibald asked with a sneer.

"Yes, there is. Look on a map."

"Mom, you said dinner is ready?" Sophie stood in the kitchen doorway.

"Cory's waiting in the cottage."

I shut off the light and bid goodnight to my supernatural friends. Sophie and I entered the cottage and were welcomed by the smell of slightly burned fish.

"I tried to keep the food warm, but you guys took forever to get here," Cory explained.

The fish was tasty, despite being overdone. Cory is an excellent cook. I guess I should keep him.

In retrospect, it was silly of me to frame the vampire problem in terms of negative publicity. But I was blissfully ignorant as we dined.

It wasn't until just before bed, when I saw the glowing, reddish eyes through the bedroom window, that I panicked.

The vampire was not supposed to enter the inn while Roderick was inside. Vampires need permission to enter another's territory. But obviously, that didn't stop her when Roderick was out feeding the other night.

And there was nothing stopping her from entering the cottage.

I grabbed a metal shish kebob skewer from the kitchen, went right up to the window and displayed the skewer to the vampire while I pressed my crucifix against the glass.

The vampire actually came closer.

In the light coming through the window from the room, she

was revealed to be young and beautiful, with bright red hair that stood out against her deathly white skin.

Her eyes stopped glowing red. In the ambient light, they were focused and intelligent—not wild and roving like those of an infected vampire.

She laughed at me, her lips stained crimson with blood.

Then, she disappeared.

I waited and listened. There were no sounds of entry, only Cory's snores coming from the bedroom. I prayed the vampire had left the area.

When I felt I could let down my guard a bit, I called Diego and told him what had happened.

"This is not good," he said.

"No kidding."

"We initially assumed that her brazen attack on your inn, and the turning of your guest, meant she was infected. We didn't think of the other possibility."

"Which is?"

"With most of the vampires of San Marcos infected, and the Fae who were to rule them withdrawing from the city, there is a huge power vacuum."

"You mean she's not from around here?"

"I believe she has come to San Marcos to be the new dominant vampire. She's turning humans to build a following. With our local vampires behaving insanely and focused only on preying upon humans, she has nothing to stop her."

"What will she do with our local vampires?"

"She'll make the uninfected ones, such as Roderick and me, submit to her. The others she will probably kill."

"Yeah, you're right. This is not good."

"The infected vampires are dangerous to me right now, but

they're still my friends. I don't want them to be destroyed. It puts that much more urgency on breaking the spell."

"And stopping this new vampire. But how?"

"The same way treacherous humans have done it for millennia: find out who she is, hunt her down, and stake her during the day."

"At least we're better off than if we were enslaved by the Fae," I said, yet again finding the bright side.

"No, we're not. This is much worse."

CHAPTER 3

FATHER OF LIES

"Just so you know, it happened again," Samson said over the phone.

"A vampire attack?"

"Yeah. Another tourist. The Tourism Board will not be happy about this."

"The victim was drained to death?"

"A young married couple had been hitting the bars and were walking along the waterfront at about three in the morning. Someone ambushed them from the shadows. The husband was knocked unconscious. When he came to, he saw his wife lying on the promenade, dead. He called nine-one-one and reported his wife had two puncture wounds in her neck. He claimed their attacker was a woman. And then it gets weird."

"Weirder, you mean. Vampire attacks are not regular cases for paramedics, even in San Marcos."

Samson laughed bitterly. "I'm afraid they soon will be. Anyway, when the ambulance got there, all they found was the husband lying on the promenade, deceased. Signs of exsanguination. His wife was nowhere to be found."

"She woke up as a vampire and bit him?"

"I'm thinking the original vampire returned to the scene, attacked the husband, then reanimated the wife as a new vampire. The two females left the husband behind to begin the new vampire's existence."

"Kind of like a chick flick."

"The story isn't over. The ambulance was taking the deceased husband to the morgue when he suddenly regained consciousness inside the ambulance."

"So, the vampire turned him, too, before she left him. Like Mr. Jubbles."

"Both paramedics were riding in the front of the ambulance. No reason for one to be in the back with a corpse. But they heard a ruckus and looked back there to see the husband jump from the rear doors. The paramedics thought they were hallucinating, but they stopped the vehicle and checked behind it. They glimpsed the victim sprinting away into an alley."

"Wow. That *is* weird."

"Things weren't this crazy, even when the vampires were infected with the spell. And after the Fae abandoned their invasion, the infected vampires were lying low. They didn't kill and turn as many of their victims. They just fed carelessly. It was difficult to explain those cases as muggings, but we managed to. Now, these attacks are so brazen."

"Because it's not a feral vampire committing them. She has a plan."

I explained Diego's theory about the new vampire usurping power in San Marcos.

"Wonderful," Samson said. "Just wonderful."

"Humans can't intervene in this vampire war. That makes it

even more critical to break the spell so Pedro and the Clan of the Eternal Night can protect their territory and restore order."

"Of course. But no one knows how to break the spell."

"The Fae can't do it. No human magician has been able to, though we're going to keep trying. I can think of only one other way to do it."

"How?"

"Somehow, make the individual who created the spell break it."

THIS TIME, IT WAS I WHO REQUESTED THE MEETING OF THE Memory Guild. Nonetheless, I had to endure yet another morality lesson while my spirit used astral travel to reach our virtual meeting hall.

Minutes after Archibald relayed my request to Dr. Noordlun, I found myself soaring high above the coastline of Florida at night. I dropped in altitude and flew over the San Marcos lighthouse, but its light had been extinguished. I continued up the coast and was surprised to see very few homes with lights on.

Gliding just above the beach like a seagull, I could look into the windows of luxurious oceanfront homes. The few that had lights burning contained scenes of debauched parties. With my enhanced senses, I knew the partiers were vampires.

The other homes I passed were abandoned and in disrepair. Further up the coast, I flew over a commercial zone. When I reached an abandoned shopping center, my heart froze.

The empty parking lot was surrounded by a tall chain-link fence topped with barbed wire. Inside was a prison camp filled with people, some beneath tattered tarps, others sleeping in the open.

I realized right away what they were: human slaves of the vampires. Livestock for feeding their masters.

This is what the future had in store for humankind?

These in-flight movies I was forced to endure during my travels to guild meetings were often more warnings than prophesies. This one couldn't have been more blatant.

With no transition, I was standing beneath the looming stone walls of our meeting hall, torches flickering high above. The members of the Memory Guild were arrayed in the circle, standing or, in Laurel's case, sitting in her wheelchair. Archibald perched on the wall six feet up.

"You requested the meeting," Dr. Noordlun said to me. "The floor is yours."

I recounted the discussion Diego and I had about the threat of not only the feral vampires, but of others taking over from them.

"The situation is dire. We will see more vampire-on-human attacks, and all will be deadly, turning the humans into vampires. Not only will this bring the existence of vampires into public knowledge, other supernaturals will be revealed, as well. And San Marcos will become a city of the dead. Maybe state and federal authorities will get involved. Maybe not. But it's shaping up to be a complete disaster.

"We must break the evil spell and free our vampires so they will stop turning humans and be capable of defending this territory against the interloping vampires."

"We've known about this spell for quite some time, and the Magic Guild could not break it," Dr. Noordlun said.

"The Faerie Queene believed Aastacki, as the Fae call him, is behind this. The Father of Lies, as we call him, is the arch nemesis of the Memory Guild. We need to use our archive of history and memory to learn more about him. He became a fallen angel before humans were on the earth, but only we of the Guild have the records of what happened. If we learn more about him, we might discover his weaknesses."

THE ARCHIVES OF THE MEMORY GUILD ARE STORED IN THE Hall of Records, a separate plane of existence apart from our planet. Think of it as the backup memory of the world. Here, the Memory Guild and our forebears have accumulated all the memories of humankind and of the earth itself before humans.

If all that information sounds impossible to fathom, I agree. It's not a collection of books or databases. It's more like a living brain with complex layers of memories organized organically, not necessarily with human logic.

In fact, the archives are contained in living creatures. When you first behold the hall, you see rows upon rows of large bookcases filled with leather-bound books. But your eyes deceive you. Each bookcase is actually a living creature called a Tugara, which is something akin to a cross between a slug, a dragon, and a plant. The Tugara have endless lifespans, but are subject to injury or accidental death, and must always be protected. Through the power of the Goddess, I gave them the ability to procreate, so if a creature was ever lost, another can absorb its memories and replace it.

After a raid on the Hall of Records by the Fae and probing of the archives by the Father of Lies, I had Sophie cast a powerful protection spell around the facility. She would need to use her magic to allow us to enter.

Dr. Noordlun met us at the Esperanza Inn. It was decided that only he and I would go to the Hall of Records to minimize the disruption.

"Rather than take down the entire protection spell and leave the hall vulnerable," Sophie said, "I'm going to give you guys a magic key. That's the easiest way to explain it."

Sophie was her normal bright self, rather than the moody mortal in love with a god. This gave me hope I wasn't losing her to Haarg.

Because she was a water witch, Sophie had five small bowls of saltwater arranged in a circle. She, Dr. Noordlun, and I stood inside it while she closed her eyes, raised her hands, and softly murmured an incantation. She was being trained by Arch Mage Bob, the most powerful magician in the region; but some of her magic she learned from the faerie Baldric. That's what concerned me. I didn't fully trust the Fae—other than Baldric—and her experimenting with Fae magic is how Sophie "met" Haarg, after all.

She pointed her hands at Dr. Noordlun and me. An electric tingling coursed through me, from my scalp to my toes.

"You'll be able to pass through the protection spell now," she told us. "And exit through it, too. I'm not sure how long this spell will last, but it will only be a matter of hours, so don't stay in the hall too long. You don't want to be trapped there."

"No, we most certainly do not," Dr. Noordlun said, grinning through his large white beard. "Thank you, Sophie."

"Are you ready?" I asked him.

"Are *you* ready? Normally, I am the one member of the guild who communicates with the Tugara to extract information. Today, we're seeking memories from before humans existed. I lack the context to even inquire about it. Your psychometry will be the best way to seek the information you want."

I gulped. "Okay." This would be much more complicated than my usual method of touching an object and experiencing the memory of a human who had touched it previously.

"I can't guarantee it will work, but I'll try."

"And succeed," he said with a reassuring smile.

Because Diana wasn't here to transport us with her astral magic, we summoned a gateway to take us to the Hall of Records. Dr. Noordlun had always had the ability to call gateways. I couldn't do so myself until recently and had depended upon their whims to show up.

So much has changed for me recently. When I assumed my role as the incarnation of Danu, I could summon gateways with ease. Then, I learned they were not phenomena of physics, but were angels. That blew my mind.

Right before we passed through the shimmering portal, I said hello to the gateway.

"How are you?" I asked.

It didn't respond. It was just an angel doing a job.

With the usual lurch of nausea, I emerged from the gateway into the Hall of Records, Dr. Noordlun right behind me.

The vast space made of marble had towering walls and a classical-style dome ringed with skylights. Arrayed across the floor in library-like rows were the Tugara. About forty feet long, twenty feet wide, and two stories tall, the Tugara had skin that resembled the spines of leather-bound books. Last time I was here, there had been twelve of them, but now I noticed a thirteenth, smaller, one.

"Oh, my goodness!" I exclaimed. "They had a baby."

"Yes. As it grows, it will absorb the information of its parents, as well as additional facts and memories. I believe an additional Tugara is pregnant now."

I approached the baby. It had the sweet, bookish scent of its species, but sweeter than that of the elders. Before I could reach it, a giant bookcase suddenly moved to block me and protect its young. I quickly retreated from the gigantic creature.

Dr. Noordlun chuckled. "The mother doesn't seem to care that it was you who gave her the ability to procreate."

"It was the Goddess who did. I hope the mother isn't the one I need to connect with."

"Allow me to make a telepathic bond with them to find out which one."

He closed his eyes and went into a trance. This was his usual way to fetch information from the archives, and he was teaching other members of the guild to do this.

"The farthest Tugara, at the end of the hall, is the one."

It was a long walk there, and when I reached the massive creature, I placed my palms against its side. It felt just like touching a row of leather books, smooth but with the evenly spaced ridges across the spines old books sometimes have.

I sensed none of the psychic energy that humans leave as residue upon the objects they touch, especially if they experienced intense emotion or highly focused thoughts while contacting the objects. I didn't expect to, of course, but that was how I was accustomed to reading memories.

No, this time it would have to be like when I touched the ground to hear the trees communicating with their root systems buried below. My psychic ability needed to penetrate the thick hide of this creature and tap into its internal psychic energy. Understanding the creature's thoughts would be unlikely, but I hoped to tap into the historic incidents the creature stored as living memories.

Going into a semi-trance state, I attempted to forge a bond with the creature's mind. Soon, I no longer felt my hands on its side. Sinking into the creature's inner essence, I received scattered images that were brief but intense.

A star forming from a pinprick of light in the darkness and

growing into a bright orb. Millions of such orbs scattered across the darkness, soaring away in every direction.

The universe was coming into existence.

The images now came to me in quick staccato bursts. Many of them I didn't understand, but they began to form a narrative that made sense to me. It was as if the Tugara—or whoever placed these memories in it—was deliberately telling me a story.

I sensed the effort of God as he performed his works, but I couldn't see him. After planets formed across the vast universe, and the most primitive creatures multiplied upon these tiny stones, highly intelligent entities came into being.

The angels.

Earlier human authors described them as an army, but they were more like God's bureaucrats, keeping a distant eye on human activities, sometimes intervening in minor ways. They oversaw God's creations across the universe and reported to the Maker of its ever-evolving beauty and richness.

Until ego and pride got in the way. These emotions are not found only in humans; intelligent animals can have them and so do the super-advanced beings called angels.

Certain individuals did not want to serve God any longer. They chafed at his commands. Some, like the one named Lucifer, wanted to take a more active role in the lives of the creatures inhabiting the universe. He wanted, in fact, to be a god himself. He had comrades who felt the same as he.

We all know how that worked out.

When the fallen angels rebelled and were cast down into Hell, one of them was the Father of Lies. This name was sometimes ascribed to Lucifer, also known as Satan. But the Father of Lies was a distinct individual, an angel who was now a demon. Western authors never gave him a human-like name, but the Father of Lies was sufficient.

My mind pushed into this narrative of memories, trying to center it around this one individual.

I got a brief glimpse of his face in human form, a bearded elderly man matching the entity I had seen in my bedroom one night. Of all the demons, the Father of Lies was most obsessed with the affairs of humans. He warped their discourse, seeding it with lies and conspiracies. He reveled in human ignorance and making people act irrationally. Harming human society in this way made him feel powerful, like the god he wished he was.

As the images, thoughts, and ideas entered my mind rapid-fire, the story of the Fae became intertwined with his. I didn't know why, until I got glimpses of a stunningly handsome faerie-like entity whom I instantly recognized as Haarg. The God of War welcomed the Father of Lies into the pantheon of Fae gods and named him Aastacki. Aastacki meddled in faerie affairs, just as he did with humans, precipitating wars and delighting Haarg.

The difference was, the Fae had lots of magic, whereas only the rare human did. The magic intoxicated Aastacki. He realized the Fae magic, amplified by his power as an angel-turned-demon, gave him immense control over the affairs of earthlings. He was nowhere as powerful as God, but his effect upon humans and the Fae was more immediate.

Just as Lucifer, the leader of the fallen angels, had wanted to be God, so did Aastacki. And the latter rejoiced in his power to sow distrust and start wars. It was a petty way to control humans, but it was enough for him. For now. What he truly wanted was for humans to adore and worship him.

This narrative of ancient history overwhelmed my brain. I struggled to make sense of it and remember what I learned. With my hands pressed against the Tugara and my consciousness in a semi-trance, I couldn't take notes. I had to remember these secrets being revealed to me.

The narrative of Aastacki faded, and I was bombarded with stories of Paleolithic humans and their slow evolution toward civilization. I tore my hands away from the leathery touch of the Tugara.

Panting, I awoke from the trance and tried to become myself again.

"Did you learn anything useful?" Dr. Noordlun asked.

"I'm not sure. Possibly. I learned a little about the Father of Lies."

"Tell me. Don't bother trying to make sense of what you experienced. Tell me quickly, before you forget."

"The Father of Lies wants to be God, just like Lucifer did. But our foe has learned how to manipulate the intelligent species with his lies. Yes, I know, this is nothing new. What I'm sensing is a petty joy in manipulating us. He doesn't care about creating universes like God. He simply revels in the immediate satisfaction of making people hate each other. Of creating rumors that lead to bloodshed. He's a small, pathetic demon who is too obsessed with humans. He is insecure—and that is his weakness. Yeah, I know I didn't discover his soft white underbelly to give us an easy win. But there must be a way to exploit his insecurity."

"Brilliant!" Dr. Noordlun said. "You did, in fact, discover a key to defeating him and breaking the spell he created. I don't know how, but we clever humans will eventually find a way."

CHAPTER 4

SOPHIE'S SPELLS

"You told me you destroyed vampires with the power the Goddess gave you," Sophie said as she flipped through a dusty old grimoire of magic spells.

"The vampires were infected. The power of the Goddess destroyed them because the evil spell had corrupted them. They were like an invasive cancer that harms vampires as a species. In the Goddess's eyes, killing them was an act of healing because it saved others. The new vampire I'm worried about is a healthy vampire. My power won't work against her and the vampires she has turned."

"Aren't *all* vampires corrupted creatures? They're supposed to be dead but they're not." Her voice had a fearful edge. You can't blame her for that. She had been kidnapped recently by a feral vampire under the command of the faerie Jaekerie. I turned the vampire into a pile of ashes. The first two vampires I destroyed, after they attacked Summer and me, left me feeling guilty. The one who had kidnapped my daughter, not so much.

"Arch Mage Bob put a warding spell on the inn. You said it

would keep vampires out, but it didn't work with the one that got Mr. Jubbles."

"Maybe it will still work with most vampires," I said, though I wasn't entirely sure. Would it work at all with non-infected vampires? "Just to be extra secure, I want you to add an extra layer of magic to protect the inn."

It was unfair of me to dump my worries on her, but I didn't want any more vampires endangering my family and guests.

Sophie's anxiety and frustration as she searched for a spell made me realize her magic evolution had made her better at destroying than protecting. It must have been the influence of the Fae magic and Haarg. It had shocked me to see her destroy the anthropophagi who had invaded the inn after entering the world through the tear in the Veil.

I had a feeling that Sophie's magic career would not be that of a typical witch.

"Oh, here's a warding spell," she said, pointing to a page in the grimoire densely packed with instructions. "It looks like a pain in the butt, and I need to collect some ingredients at the beach. I'll get on it now."

"Thank you. And please get enough ingredients to cast the spell at Grammers' house, too. She needs to be protected. The shop doesn't close until after sunset, so it would be easy for a hostile vampire to wander in."

"Of course, Mom. I'll put the same warding spell on her home."

"When will you be ready to cast it?"

"I should have all the ingredients and the spell ready to cast by the day after tomorrow."

"Good. Grammers invited us for dinner then. So, you can cast the spell here, and then we'll go to her house and do it before we eat."

My cousin Missy once told me that a witch needs courage to cast a new spell for the first time. She needs plenty of self-confidence to cast any spell, but a new one could create unexpected consequences and, if you get anything wrong, could be outright dangerous.

If there's one thing you could say about Sophie, she was courageous.

The spell-casting process was too arcane for me to understand, but I sensed a great deal of energy was consumed and produced in building and releasing the spell. She didn't make it look effortless like Bob, a highly experienced mage, did. She was super enthusiastic, though. Afterwards, she sweated like she'd just had a full workout.

"The most difficult part of this spell was making an exception for Roderick and Mr. Jubbles. It should keep out all the other vampires. I'm not completely confident Mr. Jubbles will be allowed back inside if he leaves, though. He hasn't lived here long enough for the inn to absorb enough of his energy."

"As far as I'm concerned, he's overstayed his welcome," I said. "If he gets locked out, I won't shed any tears."

"Mom, that's not nice."

"Roderick is more than enough of a vampire for our inn. Now, let's go see Grammers."

"I don't want to get all sweaty before dinner."

"You can shower off there after you cast the spell."

My mother's house smelled of roast chicken, potatoes, and rosemary. All the many lamps were on throughout the store, which had taken up the entirety of my childhood home except for the kitchen and the third floor. Mom was showing an elderly woman several rings from the glass case by the checkout table. Creaking in the ceiling meant there was still a customer or two upstairs.

I would have preferred that Mom close before dark, but this time of year, night comes early. And Mom was never one to shoo customers away, even though few of the people who paraded through here each day ever bought anything. I estimated that only twenty-five percent of the visitors here were serious buyers. The rest were tourists killing time, who would only buy something if it really grabbed them and would fit in a suitcase.

Mom excused herself from the jewelry browser and came from behind the counter to hug us both. I whispered to Mom what Sophie was going to do for her.

"Oh, that sounds splendid! If it doesn't keep any customers away."

"How many of your customers are vampires, Mom?" I asked.

"Who knows? Vampires do love antiques, after all."

"I'm going to do my, um, work, in the kitchen now," Sophie said.

Mom returned her attention to the customer, and I wandered around looking for any interesting new pieces. The parlor across the hall still had the shelves loaded with lava lamps. These have been here for years, with only a couple having been sold. But will Mom finally ditch them? Nope. It's against her instincts as a hoarder.

I continued roaming through the rooms of the first floor of what used to be a normal Victorian-era home before Dad passed away and Mom began accumulating all this stuff at a rate faster than it sold.

Oh, wait, here was something new by the foot of the stairs: a suit of armor. Its gauntleted hands grasped the hilt of a broadsword that was propped up from the floor. The visor of the helmet was closed.

"Welcome to the family," I said, knowing Sir What's-His-Name might be here gathering dust for years.

Out of curiosity, I hovered my hands above the armor, feeling for the energy of memories. Aside from Mom's, there were memories on the helm and the sword—very old ones. I picked up some thoughts of an interior decorator from the eighteen hundreds that indicated the armor was a replica—not a museum-quality original medieval suit.

I wanted to go upstairs, but someone was still browsing up there. The jewelry customer finally left, having bought nothing.

"I'm going to check on Sophie," I said, squeezing past random furniture and bric-à-brac.

Passing through the butler's pantry, I sensed a surge of supernatural energy spreading through the house. I didn't have the magic gene like Sophie, Mom, and previous generations of my family, but my psychic abilities made me sensitive to the effects of magic.

In the kitchen, the smell of dinner was currently overpowered by the scent of ozone, seaweed, sandalwood incense, and noxious herbs I couldn't identify. Sophie rose from the floor, dripping with sweat.

"I felt the spell," I said, giving her a hand.

"Yes. It has filled the house. I'm confident it will keep vampires out of here. At least, normal, non-infected vampires."

Why did this have to be so complicated? We needed to cure the infection quickly.

"I'm going upstairs to shower," Sophie said, referring to the bathroom on the third floor she used when she was living here with her grandmother.

The stairs thumped as she jogged upstairs. A creak of the

floorboards on the second floor told me the other customer was still up there. I felt uneasy about Sophie showering on the third floor while a stranger roamed around on the floor below. It would be best to check on this person.

I climbed the stairs, making plenty of noise so I wouldn't startle the customer. Junk—I mean, merchandise—was placed at the edge of each riser. A safety hazard and insurance nightmare.

The second-floor landing was no different. The bedrooms on this floor were where my parents, sister, and I lived when we were a normal family. Before Mom took up witchcraft as a hobby and hoarding as an obsession. Now, it was a disorganized jumble of used furniture, books, vinyl records, sporting goods, and just plain old weird stuff, like a fake Egyptian sarcophagus. The rooms were not organized by their category of merchandise. If you were looking for something specific, you needed to ask Mom or look in every single room.

The exception was the smallest room. It was filled with nothing but mirrors—covering the walls and stand-up mirrors arrayed around the floor.

Flashes of reflections across various mirrors told me the customer was in here, a man in his seventies.

The cliché that mirrors don't reflect vampires is not true. Here was proof: the man appearing in the mirrors was clearly a vampire—and a new one at that.

He had a look of bestial desperation from struggling with his transition. His eyes darted about nervously, wide with hunger. He did not hide his extracted fangs. His shirt wasn't tucked in, and his belly poked out. Specks of dirt covered his face and grass blades hung from his hair, most likely from when he was attacked and turned. The floor creaked beneath the faded red rug as he paced anxiously, waiting for the store to clear out so he could be alone with his prey.

Mom.

I quickly stepped out of view before he could see me. As a vampire, he could probably smell me, so I had to get out of here. He was here before we arrived and hadn't followed Sophie upstairs. I was certain that much older and easier-to-catch Mom was his intended prey. I hurried to the top of the stairs so I could go down and warn her.

The step groaned as if I had injured it.

I paused. But then I remembered he had heard me climbing the stairs and didn't attack me, so he would naturally expect to hear me descending them.

Oops, I shouldn't have paused. The vampire appeared in the doorway of the mirror room, curious about why I had stopped.

I smiled nervously at him, then continued down the stairs.

My expression must have given me away because the stairs groaned behind me as he followed.

I risked a glance back at him. He was right behind me, his tongue darting from his mouth like a hungry snake's.

"Wait," he said, reaching for me with one hand.

Thank goodness this guy hasn't learned how to mesmerize his prey yet, I thought as I sprinted down the steps as fast as I could without falling.

"A vampire is in the house!" I shrieked at the top of my lungs to warn Mom and Sophie.

And then I fell, right before reaching the bottom, crashing into the suit of armor, the armor and I clattering upon the foyer floor.

Scrambling to my feet, I saw the broadsword lying nearby and grabbed it. That and my crucifix were my only weapons.

The vampire lurched down the stairs and reached the foyer just as I was sprinting to the rear of the house. The creature was awkward in his transitioning phase, not yet having realized the preternatural speed of his new species.

Otherwise, I'd be vampire chow already.

I made it to the swinging door into the kitchen and plowed into it shoulder first like a football running back.

It was like hitting a brick wall. I stumbled backward.

"You stay out of here, you nasty vampire!" Mom warned from the other side of the door.

"Mom, it's me. Let me in!"

She stepped aside so I could push the door in and take over the task of blocking the door.

"How did you get so strong?"

"Magic and good nutrition."

"You realize the door swings out in the other direction, too, right?"

"There's no handle on that side to pull it."

The door hit me as the vampire threw himself against it. Mom joined me at the door, both of us planting our feet and putting all our weight into keeping the vampire out and ourselves alive.

"He hasn't developed his full vampire strength yet," I explained. "Still, he's too strong to hold him out much longer."

"Then what are we going to do? Use that sword on him? It's not even sharp."

"I was hoping Sophie had some magic up her sleeve that can help. Too bad she cast the warding spell to keep vampires out while he was already inside."

"The vampire is the customer who was upstairs?" Mom asked.

"Yeah."

"I just knew he wouldn't buy anything." She seemed more disgusted with him than afraid of him.

He hit the door again, harder this time. Our feet slipped backwards on the tile floor.

Our prospect for survival was slipping, too.

"Mom, do you have a cross or crucifix handy?"

"Not handy. There's a few in the jewelry case up front."

"You don't have any garden stakes in here, do you?"

"Of course not."

"What about shish kebab skewers?"

"In the drawer beneath the toast—"

The door blew open, and we went sprawling onto the floor. The sword slid across the floor in the opposite direction. We crab-walked backward away from the vampire who crouched in front of us, panting like the overweight human he used to be.

I held up my crucifix. "Stay back."

He stared at it, confused. Then tentatively moved closer.

"Back! Get back!"

Whatever power the crucifix held over him was mild. The vampire moved toward me with his mouth open and fangs gleaming.

Mom screamed. It's very unsettling to hear your mother scream in utter terror.

"He must know you haven't been to church in forever," she wailed to me.

Metal clanked from just outside the door that had swung shut. The vampire paused and looked back at the door as something pushed against it.

The door opened, and my knight in shining armor strode into the kitchen.

Actually, it was only a suit of armor, somewhat tarnished, with no knight inside.

"Is Sophie doing this?" Mom asked.

"That's my girl!"

The magically animated suit of armor marched over to the shocked vampire, swung its arm, and smacked the vampire in the head.

The vampire wasn't hurt, only shocked. But he retreated a few steps from the armor, while Mom and I crawled farther away and under the kitchen table.

Mom sniffed. "I'm worried the chicken will be overcooked. The oven's not on a timer."

"Mom! Focus on the task at hand."

The magic armor hit the vampire again so hard the suit's right arm snapped off and fell to the floor.

The vampire, encouraged, lunged at his foe. And his foe kicked him in the family jewels. Vampires can't make babies the normal way, but the kick must have hurt based on how the vampire bent over and clutched himself.

I was impressed by how well the armor-without-a-knight fought, but I doubted it would prevail.

The sword was still on the floor, unnoticed by either antagonist, but I couldn't get to it without going through them.

I made a run for the drawer to get the skewers.

The vampire caught the sleeve of my blouse, and I lost my footing. The armor stepped in front of me right before the vampire could seize me. He collided with the knight with a metallic clang. The helm fell off the suit, landing on my foot.

The door burst open, and Sophie ran in. Her hair was still wet from the shower, and her eyes were bright with excitement and magic.

"There's a sword on the floor to your left," I told her, remembering that she used one with her magic when she fought the anthropophagi and made their brains literally explode.

She found it and held it in both hands, pointing it at the vampire as she crouched, ready to spring.

The sword glowed, radiating a purple aura.

The vampire hesitated. The suit of armor stood, frozen.

Sophie mouthed silent words.

The vampire leaped at her before a blast of purple lightning shot from the sword blade and hit him, throwing him onto the kitchen counter, knocking the toaster aside.

Another bolt of purple lightning hit the creature, consuming it in purple flames.

Soon, nothing but a pile of ashes atop the counter was left of the vampire.

Sophie breathed a sigh of relief, and the sword stopped glowing. The suit of armor collapsed onto the floor.

Mom raced to the oven and turned it off. Opening the door, she stuck a meat thermometer into the bird.

"Perfect!" she said, beaming, putting on oven mitts to remove the roasting pan.

"I didn't realize I'd trap a vampire *in* the house when I cast the warding spell," Sophie said. "That was awkward."

"Well, there's no vampire here anymore," I replied, walking over to give her a hug.

"Thanks for rescuing us, dear," Mom said. "I wonder, is it safe to remove vampire ashes with a vacuum cleaner?"

I studied Sophie with pride and amazement. The young woman who had defeated substance abuse disorder, yet had seemed aimless career-wise, shined with power and potential.

What did destiny have in store for my daughter?

CHAPTER 5

WAR-GOD BOYFRIEND

"So, Sophie, any new men in your life?" Mom asked, as her magic sent the levitating platter of carved chicken floating to each of us.

"Mom!" I scolded. "We were nearly killed by a vampire who was here to prey upon you. Sophie destroyed him with a destructive power I've never seen produced by a witch before. And you're asking about dating?"

"He's dreamy," Sophie said.

"What does he do for a living?" Mom asked, ignoring me.

"Um, he's in sales."

"In a high-paying field, I hope? Stocks? Technology?"

"War."

"Oh, he's with a defense contractor? He's probably rich."

"He's the Fae God of War. His name is Haarg. I can't wait for you to meet him, though he might not be ready for that step yet."

I kept my mouth shut and searched Mom's face for her reaction.

43

"My word. This family certainly has its share of divinities."
She cast a sardonic look at me.

"It wasn't my choice to be the personification of Danu," I
said.

"Sophie, do you think it's a good idea to date a god of war
when your mother is the earth mother?"

"I can't help it if Mom approves of my boyfriends or not."

"I never said I didn't approve of him. But I represent life and
healing. He is a force of death and destruction."

"That's not a nice thing to say."

"He's the god of *war*, for Pete's sake. It was partly because of
him that the Fae were invading San Marcos."

"It's not because of him. He was just a mascot of sorts."

"How did you meet this gentleman?" Mom asked.

"When Baldric was teaching me magic, some spells invoked
the power of Haarg. Which made him notice me. He found me
attractive. Then, he began to visit me in spirit form."

"This sounds like the kind of thing Zeus used to do," Mom
said. "Next thing you know, Sophie will be pregnant or turn into
a heifer."

"My worries exactly," I said.

"You guys aren't even giving him a chance."

"It doesn't matter what we think. You're a grown woman and
can date whomever you want. And he's a god. He'll take
whomever he wants."

"You're so unromantic."

I sighed. The gravy boat had been hovering above my plate,
so I poured some on my chicken and gave it a push in Sophie's
direction. "The weather sure has been nice."

"Yes," Mom said. "No more of that brutal humidity."

"Haarg isn't all about violence, you know," Sophie said with a
pout. "He has a tender side. He celebrates the close bond

44

between comrades-in-arms and mourns the loss of those who have fallen."

"Now, *that's* romantic." I didn't mean it to sound as sarcastic as it did.

Sophie glowered as she picked at her roasted potatoes.

"Well, thank you for the warding spell," Mom said to her. "I would hate to keep out a vampire who wants to spend a lot of money here, but it's better safe than sorry."

"No offense, Mom. But the vampires I know would only buy high-end antiques. Except for Roderick, of course, who's broke. Not that they're going to shop for interior decor while they're insane from the evil spell. Or, freshly turned into vampires."

"It sounds like the vampire problem in San Marcos has only gotten worse."

"It has."

"Are you going to do something about it?"

"Mom, I'm not the mayor of San Marcos, nor am I on the Executive Council of the Guilds. I'm just an innkeeper."

"You're allegedly a goddess." She sounded jealous.

"I sure hope the pleasant weather sticks around for the rest of the week."

For several minutes, the only sounds were the clinking of cutlery on plates.

"When you're ready, I'd like to meet your special war-god friend," Mom said to Sophie.

Sophie nodded with a skeptical expression.

WHEN SOPHIE AND I RETURNED TO THE INN, DIEGO WAS outside waiting for us.

"Darla, I need to show you something," he said darkly. "Please come with me."

I nodded to Sophie that it was okay for her to go inside, then I climbed into the passenger seat of Diego's 1968 Aston Martin.

As the car rumbled down narrow cobblestone streets, I resisted the urge to ask him where we were going. The anger on his face warned me against it.

"Our destination is quite near," he said, as if reading my thoughts.

His thoughts, though, were unreadable to me, as was the case with many vampires. And maybe that's a good thing. The random thoughts of the undead were probably freaky.

Diego downshifted, then parked at the curb in front of a run-down home. The nearest streetlight wasn't working, so this section of the block was extra dark, with only the faint light from a crescent moon illuminating it.

The house was a narrow, two-story clapboard, a Gothic Revival from the mid-nineteenth century, with an ornamental scrollwork in the fascia below the peak of the roof. The windows were all shuttered, except one of the two windows upstairs had a shutter with a broken upper hinge, so it hung open at an angle, like one eye blinking.

I sensed remnants of supernatural energy in the home.

"Is this a vampire nest?" I asked.

Diego nodded. "A small one. Come inside. It's safe now."

I followed him up the front-porch stairs. The wooden screen door was missing its screens. The front door behind it was unlocked. We entered the small front parlor.

Diego handed me a flashlight that he didn't need.

"Go ahead," he said. "Look around."

I shined the light around the sparsely furnished room.

There had been a massacre here.

I found five sets of clothing spread on the floor. It was as if whoever had been wearing them simply disappeared from their clothing, but they hadn't fully disappeared. They left piles of dust behind after their undead bodies had been destroyed.

Two other bodies were in less advanced stages of decay. One was a mummified corpse. The other was a skeleton with a pile of hair near the skull.

The older a vampire is, the more decayed her body is when she is destroyed. The body of a 500-year-old vampire becomes what it would be if it had lain in a grave for 500 years.

"There are two more upstairs," Diego said. "I happened to be driving down this street when I sensed that several of my kind had been lost. This house has been a nest for over a century, and all the vampires in it were infected by the spell. They've kept a low profile ever since the Fae left town."

"Did humans destroy them? Or the new vampires?"

"Humans didn't do this. I see no signs of stakes or tools for beheading. And look at their clothing."

He pointed to the nearest bodies. The clothing, both men's and women's, appeared to have been sliced open with claws.

"Executed by the new vampires," I whispered.

Diego nodded.

I shut off the flashlight and turned to face the door.

"Don't worry. The invaders aren't anywhere nearby. I brought you here to see if they left any memories. We need clues for tracking them down and stopping them."

The fact my telepathy didn't do well at penetrating a vampire's consciousness didn't mean my psychometry wasn't effective. Psychic energy left upon an object was still energy, though it differed from a living human's.

I looked around the room. There wasn't much here that

intruders would have handled. They did all the work with their claws.

The most obvious place to begin was the front doorknob.

Doorknobs and handles receive a lot of touching, almost always for only brief moments. The nine vampires who had resided here for more than a century handled this hardware nightly when going out to, and returning from, hunts and other errands.

Only fragments of memories remained on the cheap metal knob. It looked new, like it had been replaced, and the memories it held were all recent.

The memories were of poverty and privation. Not all vampires were wealthy bon vivants like Diego, Pedro, and other leading citizens. Nine creatures crowded into this small house because they couldn't afford any better. Many of the thoughts I picked up were work related. Some residents had jobs at night. I sensed one was a security guard. Another had the overnight shift at a convenience store. Dangerous jobs for humans, but not for vampires who didn't need to fear being shot by a robber.

Dancing my fingers upon the faux brass, I tried to isolate the most recent energy. I sensed the dark anger of Diego when he first came here, before bringing me. I searched backwards from there.

Brief but intense energy full of violent intent—that must be from one of the killers. I was no expert on vampires, but even I could tell a newly turned vampire had recently turned the knob. A male full of bloodlust. Even more recent than that, yet prior to Diego's energy, had been the touch of a mature individual, calm but full of intent and hope.

Hope—that was odd.

I couldn't get anything valuable from the doorknob. No surprise.

While I stood there, the wooden frame of the screen door was wide open, folded back against the clapboard exterior; the spring that pulled it closed had long ago rusted and snapped in two. The door shifted slightly in the breeze.

I hovered my hand over the section of the frame where Diego had grasped it. I surmised everyone grabbed the door at this location because the white paint was faded here from repeated handling.

I picked up recent energy—fleeting thoughts of someone holding the door open while watching someone else wrench the locked main door open with brute force. This individual, like the other one, was full of unbridled excitement and a hunger for violence.

Wood doesn't hold memories as well as metal, stone, and other hard surfaces do. I couldn't get any energy strong enough to send me into a reverie. And, to tell the truth, I didn't want to be sucked into the memories of a newly turned vampire who was here to create carnage.

I swung the screen door closed and noticed the small steel handle mounted lower on the frame. It was rusty and fragile looking. The portion of the frame that so many hands had grabbed once the screen was missing was at a more natural height for handling the door.

But the tiny handle held recent energy. Intense energy. I tentatively touched the metal with my finger to—

—search the place for my bangle. I can't believe how careless I was to have lost it. Wait, don't move until that car passes by. Last night was such a busy night of turning new vampires. By the time we got here, I felt drunk from over-feeding. Okay, the car is gone. It should be easy searching here with everyone destroyed—

—The memory cut off when the vampire released the handle to reach for the doorknob of the main door.

I was certain the memory had come from the experienced, powerful vampire who had turned Mr. Jubbles and, apparently, embarked on a mission to be the dominant vampire in the city.

"It's her," I said to Diego when I went back inside. He was standing by the fireplace, keeping his eyes away from the vampire remains. "She returned here to search for her bracelet, thinking she lost it here during the slaughter. But she lost it at the inn."

"You have it?"

"Actually, Detective Samson took it for fingerprinting."

"You must get it back and read it for memories."

I knew he would say that. When Samson took it, I was happy to see it leave the inn. I wanted nothing to do with that vampire and hadn't known we'd be tracking her down.

"Yes. I'll read it. It's obviously very important to her. But, while we're here, let me see if I can find any other memories."

Searching an entire house for memories is a daunting task. Think of all the surfaces and objects you touch in your own home. And out of all the memories here, very few would be helpful to us.

Before I got overwhelmed, I forced myself to think like an intruder on a mission to attack the inhabitants.

Fact is, the intruders might have touched nothing other than their victims.

"Don't vampires need permission to enter another vampire's home?" I asked Diego.

"You need permission entering vampires' territory as part of our code of ethics. If you don't get permission, they have the right to kill you. In this case, the point is moot."

"I see."

Looking around the living room and the remains of the

vampires, I envisioned the intruders bursting in without warning and immediately attacking the residents.

My eyes settled on a TV remote lying on the floor beside an overturned coffee table. The furnishings were sparse, but the house had a TV just like every human home did.

I picked up the remote and immediately sensed—

—the redhead is the oldest and most powerful vampire I've ever seen. She's killing everyone! "Where does Pedro live?" she's asking me, and grabs—

—The last thought of the male vampire who held the remote was of the female vampire grabbing his throat.

"I found memories of one victim," I said and described them.

Diego nodded. "Yes, only an elder would have the arrogance to take over another's territory. Pedro, as you know, is no longer living at his home. She obviously wants to find and destroy him."

"Too bad we don't know where he is, either."

I moved to the narrow stairs and hovered my hand over the wooden banister. Yes, one of the residents fled up the stairs terrified. I picked up quick images of the attack, but nothing coherent.

The second floor consisted of three small bedrooms and a bath. The door of one bedroom was closed. No fresh energy was on the doorknob. I opened the door. The room was empty. It was the one with the loose shutter. Rather than fix the shutter, they simply avoided the room.

A larger bedroom in the rear had two sets of clothing, and two piles of ashes, on its floor.

I had to push myself to step into that room. I mean, there were the remains of two vampires in there. Who in their right mind would go in?

Me, of course. Though I doubted I was in my right mind.

The room has four single beds and a small fireplace.

There was intense energy coming from the fireplace.

I stepped around the remains to get to the fireplace. The energy came from the mantel. I held my hand close to it, but as if the energy was a magnet, my hand was pulled to the—

—*mantel, leaning against it insouciantly while my new children toy with the infected vampires. I don't know what kind of magic was the undoing of the vampires in this town, but it was powerful. Thankfully, it's no longer contagious. It turned everyone into idiots. Animals. It's as if they need someone to tell them what to do. Perhaps instead of slaughtering them all, I can command them. But I don't know how to get through their thick skulls. Every time I ask them where Pedro is staying, they stare at me blankly, like I asked them to explain the theory of relativity. "I'm done with these morons," I tell my children. And they finish the job, rather mercifully, I would say.*

Well, the night is getting on. We've caused enough mayhem for now. Since Pedro is no longer staying at his home, I think I'll use that as my new nest. Maybe I'll get lucky, and he'll show up there and—

—she stepped away from the mantel, and the memory ended.

I felt queasy after watching her vampire children destroy the infected ones. Let's just say it involved their hearts, and while it was fast, it didn't seem so merciful to me.

DIEGO LOOKED AT ME WITH ADMIRATION. "YOUR GIFT IS remarkable."

"I don't think of it as a gift."

"Now we know where to find this invading vampire. But she's an elder. Nearly impossible to destroy. I wonder, what brought her to San Marcos?"

"Did she sense the power vacuum after the Fae withdrew their armies?"

"Oh, she sensed it as soon as she arrived, of course. But I doubt she heard about the Fae's invasion before that. And it sounds as if she didn't have prior knowledge of the infections until she saw the afflicted. Something else brought her here."

"How are we going to stop her if she's so powerful?"

It occurred to me that if we could only break the spell that infected the vampires of our city, the healed vampires could help us stop her. Right now, all we had were Diego, Roderick, and a bunch of humans. Plus, a gargoyle, for whatever he's worth. And the other supernatural guilds, assuming they would have any interest in a power struggle among vampires.

Diego came to the same conclusion. "We must enlist the other guilds."

"Good luck with that."

"First, we must check if she is living in Pedro's house now. The memories you read are days old by now, but she may not have moved in yet. Let's drive there, and I'll try to sense if she's around."

It was the last thing I wanted to do. On a prior visit there to retrieve the mysterious box that had contained the evil spell, I was attacked by an infected vampire.

I kept my mouth shut and rode with Diego after he promised we would keep our distance from the house.

"A vampire that powerful will be detectable from afar. By me, of course. Not by you, a human."

"That's why humans are your prey."

My snarky comment made me a little uncomfortable, reminding me I was like a mouse hanging out with a boa constrictor, even if we were friends. I hoped Diego had already eaten well tonight.

We traveled on a road that paralleled the Sangre River and its salt marshes, south of where it met the ocean inlet. Before long, Diego pulled over to the side of the road near the gates at the end of Pedro's winding oak-lined driveway.

"We're out of view of the surveillance cameras here."

"Do you sense her here? If so, I'm sure she can sense you."

"She's not here now. And I don't sense that she's been spending time on the property."

"Well, let's get out of here. Just the thought of her makes me nervous."

Diego turned his sports car around. As it growled back to the city, I was relieved the vampire wasn't there. I agree she needs to be stopped, but I didn't want to be involved in stopping her. I had no dog in this fight.

Or so I thought.

Diego dropped me off at the inn past midnight, and I quickly landed on the bed like a fallen tree beside my sleeping husband.

Cory had stayed behind to manage the inn while Sophie and I had gone to Mom's for dinner. I assumed Sophie had told him about the vampire who had pretended to be a customer.

That meant when I woke up, I would have to be extra sweet to him to stave off his tirade about my putting our family in supernatural danger yet again. The vampire in the antique shop was not my fault but try telling that to Cory.

Waking up before everyone else as usual, I left the cottage to enter the inn and prepare breakfast for my guests—plus a special one for Cory.

A small envelope of heavy-stock paper was stuck in the cottage door. I removed and opened the envelope, pulling out a small note card. The fancy calligraphy-style handwriting read:

"You have been looking for me. And I, you. I found you, of course, days ago when I preyed upon your guest. I look forward to making formal introductions soon."

Oh boy. Now, this *was* my fault, though I did not know why.

CHAPTER 6

THE EQUILIBRIUM

I was the special witness invited to testify before the Executive Council of the Guilds. The Memory Guild, Magic Guild, Shifter Guild, Guild of Fae and Wee People, Troll and Gnome Alliance, Elven League, and Psychic Guild were there. Even the Union of Undead Flesh Eaters was there—and that's saying a lot, because zombies and ghouls are known for erratic attendance.

The only guild that was missing, of course, was the Clan of the Eternal Night. Diego was there as its only sane member, but he wasn't its leader and thus couldn't vote with the council.

I patiently explained the deadly threat posed by the elder vampire, whose name I still did not know. And, as I expected, the other guild presidents were not as concerned as they should be.

"It sounds like she's doing us a favor. We can't break the spell that infects the vampires," said Rufus, Alpha of the Shifter Guild, "but she'll cull their population instead."

It took a troll, a faerie, and Arch Mage Bob to pry Diego's hands from Rufus' throat.

"You're a monster!" Diego shouted at him.

"We're all monsters in our own ways," Baldric said. "Sometimes, we must make cold calculations to ensure the survival of the greater whole of us."

Rufus tried to say something, but it came out as a choking cough.

"With all due respect, this calculation is misguided," I said. "You're basing it on the original purpose of the evil spell: to make us all enslaved by the Fae. The infected vampires would be commanded by the Fae directly, and they would turn humans and other species, making them also enslaved.

"But after the Fae halted their invasion," I continued, "the infected vampires stopped being such a threat to us. This new vampire, though, is deliberately turning humans to serve as her army. She's doing the same thing we were originally concerned about with the infected vampires."

"As one of the few humans here, I'm alarmed by what Darla is telling us," Bob said.

"The main purpose of the guilds, and this council, is to avoid upsetting the equilibrium," said Dr. Noordlun. "If it becomes common knowledge in the city that vampires exist and are attacking humans, we're all in grave peril."

The attendees grumbled in agreement. It was frustrating to be forced to balance on the tightrope between allowing supernaturals to flourish while keeping their true natures secret. But that was the world we lived in. In other places and times, we would be forced to hide and repress our true identities, or else be hunted down and exterminated, burned at the stake, or impaled on one.

San Marcos proves that everyone—from humans with paranormal abilities to scary-looking trolls—can live full lives. We can't reveal our true selves to everyone, but we have sophisticated networks to support us, protect us, and ensure we're never alone.

If we maintain the equilibrium.

"How do you suggest we solve this problem?" Baldric asked me.

"Work together to drive the elder vampire from our city."

"Can't we just stake her?"

"A vampire of her age and power is exceedingly difficult to destroy," Diego said coldly.

Diego was nearly 500 years old. If he considered himself weak compared to her, I can't imagine how old she was.

"And Arch Mage Bob, I need you to work with Dr. Noordlun, Sophie, and me to develop magic to break the evil spell," I implored.

"Dude, I've already told you I don't have the ability."

"We are gaining insights on the Father of Lies," Dr. Noordlun said. "They might help us."

Bob shrugged. "No harm in trying."

"In the meantime, we need to monitor the home belonging to Pedro. We think the elder vampire will move in."

"The Shifter Guild will provide scouts," said Rufus in a scratchy voice.

Diego nodded his thanks.

Then the council moved on to other important business, such as planning the annual holiday party.

I WAS WRITING A SHOPPING LIST IN THE INN'S KITCHEN WHEN I heard the pop of a piece of wood paneling being removed, then the squeaking wheels of the smaller of the two refrigerators as the appliance shuddered and moved slowly away from the wall.

A normal person would scream with fright and run from the room. As you well know, I am not normal.

"Good evening, Roderick," I said.

The appliance moved further from the wall. Finally, Roderick appeared from behind it, rubbing his face with both hands. He wore a nineteenth century dressing gown.

"I didn't expect to see you in here at this frightfully early hour," he said.

"Such a warm welcome."

"I don't like to be seen before my morning ablutions."

I stared at the opening to his crawlspace, revealed by the displaced fridge.

"Where is Mr. Jubbles?"

"Thankfully, the dullard has moved on."

"Really? Where?"

"He was summoned by his maker the night before. At last, I have my chamber to myself again."

I admit I was secretly happy Mr. Jubbles left the inn. Even though he had been sharing Roderick's crawlspace during his difficult transition to vampire—treating Roderick as a kind of adoptive parent—I had kept Mr. Jubbles' room unoccupied in case he needed it. Now, I could clear his belongings out and book the room to paying guests. The room the Fae priest Wilference had messed up so thoroughly was finally clean and occupied by a couple from Ohio. The Honeymoon Suite, where the Faerie Queene and her retinue had stayed, still needed a lot of work.

"Do you think he'll return?" I asked.

Roderick shrugged. "He appeared to be mesmerized. Somehow, his maker seized his mind from afar, and commanded him to travel to her. We were in the middle of playing checkers when his eyes rolled up in his head, and he said, 'Yes, mother, I am coming.' He stood up, walked out of the room and out the front door."

"Do you know where he went?"

"I don't have the foggiest idea."

The shifter scouts had sent no reports yet of the elder vampire being spotted at Pedro's home. Perhaps Diego and I driving there had told her it was too obvious a place for her to stay. I didn't know how she knew we went there, because Diego hadn't felt her presence, but her ability to summon Mr. Jubbles from afar proved she had powers beyond those of an ordinary vampire.

We needed to learn more about her. I texted Samson, asking him to return the bracelet. I wanted to read it if I could.

Samson called and told me he only just now got the finger-print results from forensics.

"It was low priority because it wasn't part of an actual investigation. Being, you know, a vampire attack."

"Yes, yes, but was there a match?"

"Afraid not. I'll bring the bracelet over in the morning."

As much as I was eager to find the vampire and drive her from the city, I wasn't exactly looking forward to reading her memories. After all, vampires do a lot of scary stuff.

NOT BEING FOND OF SNAKES, I FOUND IT DIFFICULT TO admire the elegance and craftsmanship of the golden double-coiled snake, its tilted head protruding from above the coil, the end of its tail looping over the coils with its tip extending out.

Grooves portrayed rings along the snake's length. The snake's eyes were blank but hinted of malice.

The bracelet seemed very ancient. Regardless of the weight of its gold, it would fetch an enormous price. I sensed centuries of memories in it. Whether I could read them was another question.

The bracelet would have always touched the skin of its owner, except when moving her arm would cause the loosely fitted piece to lose contact with her skin as it shifted. But that doesn't mean it would hold vivid memories. The best ones come from the touch of hands, lips, tongues, and other parts of our bodies we focus our attention upon.

Nevertheless, a bangle like this would often rest on the bottom of the hand. And the wearer would surely touch or fidget with it now and then.

I realized I was delaying doing my reading. Yeah, the thought of being sucked into a reverie was scaring me. It was time to take the plunge.

I sat at the desk of the cottage's second bedroom, the bracelet lying before me. It was after breakfast service, one of my few times I could be alone and undistracted. Sophie was alternating between the front desk and helping the housekeeper. Cory was doing maintenance in the courtyard. In here, it was just me and the golden snake.

And Lethia—that was her name. I held my index finger a millimeter above the bracelet, feeling the sizzle of psychic energy, when the name popped into my head.

Lethia.

She was turned as a young woman who had been widowed and lonely, realizing only when it was too late that the handsome warrior was seducing her not out of love, but out of lust and the thrill of conquest. Peer pressure convinced him to marry her.

They had a child, a girl, but the father never knew her. He went off on a raiding party and was killed in battle. She cared for her child with the help of the women in her village.

Until she died. And was brought back as a vampire.

A vampire's making is both traumatic and formative, a memory that is always just below the surface of her thoughts. But I wished to learn more specifics. I searched for the most recent memories. And there, a glimpse of—

—the human incarnation of Danu, standing by the window, speaking with someone. I must crouch behind the shrubbery in case she glances outside. It would be so easy to walk inside and register as a guest. That way, I would have many opportunities, but I'm afraid she'll know that I'm a vampire. The goddess might even remember me from before, though I doubt it.

She leaves the main building and enters a small structure in the courtyard. That is where she sleeps? The Goddess in such a humble abode? There is another human in there with her—a husband. I wait and watch until the lights go out.

How do I deal with her? I must be especially careful, as she might not succumb to mesmerizing. I could be direct. Or, I could play upon her fears.

Footsteps approaching along the sidewalk—the irregular shuffling of a drunk man. I sink into the shadows of the bushes as he staggers past me. An older, corpulent man whose stomach growls with hunger. He uses a card key to unlock the front door and enters. I slip through the door behind him before it closes.

The man enters the kitchen. Light flares when he opens a large refrigerator and then a smaller one. He mumbles something and leaves the room, halting in front of a closet door. Opening the door, he goes inside. And I have an idea.

I will begin building my army with Danu's guest. Thusly, I will pull her into my world. And my wishes.

I enter the closet silently. He is so focused on opening a container of nuts that he is not aware of me at all, leaving his neck deliciously exposed, and I—

—yanked my finger from the bracelet. I didn't need to share her experience of feeding upon and draining Mr. Jubbles, thank you kindly.

And I did not enjoy knowing Lethia was fixated on me, seemingly because of the Goddess. What does she want from me? To kill me for revenge? To turn me into the world's first earth-mother-slash-vampire? Now *that* is an oxymoron if I ever heard one.

Let this serve as another example of how being the human incarnation of a goddess isn't all it's cracked up to be.

I didn't want to spend any more time with this vampire's memories, but I wanted to find clues as to her whereabouts. Obviously, she lost the bracelet when she attacked Mr. Jubbles. However, maybe I could find out where she slept during the day before that.

I made contact again with her psychic energy, using the technique of remaining just above the memories, perusing them like the index of a book. Of course, memories aren't organized alphabetically. Nor, as you'd expect, are they in chronological order. They were, in fact, a jumble of words, images, and emotions—some leaping from the page with their intensity and others almost hidden beneath stronger memories.

It requires intuition to scan through innumerable memories and find what you're looking for. The intuition comes from practice. And I've had a great deal of it.

The number of memories attached to this bracelet was overwhelming. And these were only a tiny fraction of the vampire's total memories.

She was so old—no, I'm not going to make a mother-in-law

joke—that she wasn't using hyperbole when she thought about knowing Danu. Lethia actually existed many thousands of years ago.

I have sensed this immense span of years in the goddess who dwells within me. The thought of an actual creature being that old was astounding.

However, I sought the memories of a few short days ago— not those that survived millennia.

There was a fresh image of waking up after the setting sun had finally bled from the sky. She was in a dwelling of some sort. I touched—

—the cold skin of my victim, an old woman so confused with dementia that I couldn't bring myself to turn her and condemn her to an eternity of suffering in her condition. But I shouldn't have drained her, either. A breech of self-discipline it was, my hunger so intense I could not stop myself from feeding before I had completely emptied her. Tonight, I must be more careful and feed discreetly. Or turn someone who will serve me as I need.

I sit in the small room and fiddle with my bracelet resting on the heel of my palm, the blank eyes of the snake belying the power that lives in this trinket the goldsmith created. He was a handsome one, from the village beyond the moors. He knew I had a child and wouldn't let me take him for a roll in the hay. That was when the bracelet was just jewelry and not enchanted with magic. Enough of this nostalgia. I—

—snapped out of it as she raised her hands to her hair and the bracelet slipped down her forearm, breaking the train of memory.

I was so frustrated! The memory I just read was very recent, and it's possible Lethia is still staying at the same home.

Rushing to capture another memory from the same night, I touched the bracelet a little too quickly. The memory I was falling into was not what—

—he demanded of me. To rise from the dead for such a high price? I was foolish, but he was too cunning. His words were tempting. They were kind. They were reassuring. And now, I know they were also lies.

Evil lies.

For I did not receive eternal life. Instead, I got an existence of being dead, but not dead. Of passing through the Veil and returning to the world. But not truly being a part of it.

And Yena did not rise with me. Death wouldn't give her up.

I will forever be an outsider and an outcast, walking the earth alone and creating fear in every person I encounter.

Because I must feed on their blood to remain in this cursed existence.

If I refuse to feed, I will die. My death, he said, will be worse than when my human life ended. Now, ending my existence will give me the agony of a thousand deaths, and my suffering will last a thousand years. At the end, I will not go to the Shadowlands where my ancestors dwell. I will be alone in utter nothingness.

He laughed when he said this will not happen, because I could never refuse to feed. The hunger for blood will be greater than any hunger I have ever experienced.

I won't refuse to drink blood because I will crave it too much, he said. And I will love it.

He was right: feeding on blood is the only joy I find in my undead existence.

This god, or demon, lied to me. He didn't tell me about the price I would pay to be raised from the dead. I never would have agreed if I had known that to defeat death meant being a child of death.

Death is my mother. And this god, or demon, said he is now my father.

The Father of Lies.

He said I am the first of my kind. And my kind will be called vampire.

The only way to salve my loneliness, he said, will be to enjoy his company. And the company of others of my kind. And the only way to do that will be to make more vampires.

He told me how to make them. Can I believe him? Is this yet another lie?

I feel the power in the gold of my bracelet. It warms my hand as I touch it. The power will help me do what I must.

And so, I rise again from my funeral bed to do what I must to—

—get out of this memory. Finally, it ends as I manage to yank my hand from the bracelet and snap out of my reverie.

That was horrifying, because beyond the words that Lethia was thinking, I experienced her feelings of awakening from death. The remnants of death were in me, like the tendrils of sleep that cling to you when you first wake. I had a glimpse of the darkness she escaped, as well as the horror of the undead existence she faced.

And while she thought about her situation, she pictured the face of the demon who had brought her back to life.

The Father of Lies.

I had met him once, briefly, when he appeared in my bedroom disguised as Cory. After he abandoned his disguise, he revealed a bit of his true self.

But it was nothing like this. The entity that Lethia had seen was stomach-churning in its disgustingness while being horrifying in its existential terror.

The glowing embers in the eye sockets, the yawning pit of the open mouth.

I simply can't describe her memory of the Father of Lies. And he only revealed himself to her after she realized he had lied to her when he said she could return to life and be exactly as she was before the fever killed her.

He had duped her, because she had wanted so badly to believe him—to believe something too good to be true.

Isn't that the story of humankind? We believe in fallacies that seem ridiculous to others and are tragic when we view them in retrospect.

Yet the Father of Lies manipulates us all, some more than others, but always making the story of humans about folly, wars, and hatred that taint the good things humans do.

How I wished the Father of Lies could be forever defeated.

That, I know, will never happen. But I will do everything I can to beat him in one specific way.

By breaking the spell that infects the vampires. They were all the descendants of the very first vampire whom the Father of Lies himself created.

CHAPTER 7

MONSTER MAYHEM

I didn't want to get sucked into another reverie immersed in Lethia's memories. Try as I might, I couldn't find the location of where she was staying. Her thousands of years of memories kept pulling me back to her early days in ancient Ireland before the Gaels arrived on the island.

Images of writhing snakes kept appearing. No, there were never snakes in Ireland, even before St. Patrick showed up. What was the significance of snakes to Lethia that caused her to order a bracelet made with a snake motif? The bracelet was hers before she was turned, I was certain.

Lethia's existence was a lonely one throughout her thousands of years, despite all the vampires she turned. I saw so many memories of fog-enshrouded nights in cold, wet bogs or on rocky crags above crashing waves while ancient monsters—long since extinct—hunted. She knew they would be too fearful of attacking this undead creature unfamiliar to them.

Her only happy memories were of burying her fangs in the necks of victims who lived in an era before vampires were heard of. And she cherished being the mother of a growing nest of vampires she turned. Later, of course, her vampires turned others, and the others did so, too.

The population of vampires grew and spread around the world.

So why was Lethia alone now in San Marcos, having to create new followers? What happened to her original children?

Perhaps, like humans, vampires can grow apart over the years. Especially over centuries and millennia. Still, a vampire as old and powerful as Lethia should have arrived in San Marcos with an army already formed.

Why was she alone, except for Mr. Jubbles and the others she had recently turned?

Reading these memories was too much for me. I pulled my hands away from the bracelet and slid my chair back from the desk.

Perhaps magic could help me locate Lethia.

And I knew just the person who could help me. My cousin, Missy. I gave her a ring.

"She turned your guest? Oh, my."

"Yes," I replied. "And she's working her way through the humans of San Marcos to build an army of vampires loyal to her. She'll exterminate the infected vampires and become the vampire queen."

"Oh, my. The vampires down here are nothing like that."

"They're not like that up here, either," I said. "Whether they were seniors when they were turned, like the vampires you know, or younger in body age, the vampires of San Marcos are law-abiding and discreet. Until the evil spell infected them, that is."

"Have you had any luck in breaking the spell?"

"No. I called you to ask if you could use your locator spell to find the senior vampire. And maybe you can help us with the infection, too."

"I'll be happy to drive up there and cast my locator spell. It would be great to see you—it's been a while. But I doubt I can help with the infection. Arch Mage Bob is much more powerful than I am, and if he can't help you, I doubt I can."

"He's working on a new spell. We'll see how that works. And please come up as soon as you can. I don't know of any witch with a locator spell as good as yours. Maybe Bob has one, but he's too busy now."

"Okay. I'll rearrange my schedule and see you this weekend."

I'VE ALWAYS TENDED TO HAVE TOO MANY IRONS IN THE FIRE. For instance, while running a historic inn is enough to keep anyone busy, my psychometry and membership in the Memory Guild constantly throw complications in my way. Then, there's the goddess thing. Being divine is a full-time job, whether you're a goddess or a demigoddess. It's no hobby, believe me.

As you know, I've also been up to my eyeballs in vampire problems—from the infected bloodsuckers to Lethia.

But there is one additional problem hanging over my head, like the Sword of Damocles. I had almost forgotten about it until Samson called me later that night.

"Looks like the Veil still has a hole in it," he said.

"Everyone seems to think I'm going to get it repaired, and unless you know of someone hiring a contractor to repair it, yes, the Veil still is torn open. What kind of mythological creature came through this time?"

"Based on the hysterical chatter on the police radio, I would say it's a cyclops. What are you going to do about it?"

"I'm going to enjoy the fact it's not coming after me this time."

Since the demise of Jaekeree, the faerie who had used magic to direct creatures that came through the Veil to kill me, they now were free to kill whomever they wanted. It was a terrible situation for San Marcos, but a notable improvement for Darla Chesswick.

"Seriously," I said, "my goddess abilities are for healing, not killing. Viruses and infected vampires, I can kill. I don't believe a cyclops is an existential threat to our or its own species."

"It ate a security guard."

I sighed. "Where is it?"

"He—it's a male—apparently swam from the ocean through the inlet and across the bay, landing near the fort. It's inside the walls right now. If the fort hadn't been closed for the night, there would be lots of dead tourists. Dead tourists aren't good for the local economy."

"Tell me about it. I recently lost a guest to a vampire."

"Will you help me or not? I'm not asking you in your goddess role. I'm asking a fellow supernatural to help me solve this problem before the news media finds out about it."

"I'll meet you at the entrance to the grounds. And I'll bring Sophie with me."

Having seen her make short work of the anthropophagi at the inn and the vampire in Mom's house, I figured she was our best bet for getting rid of our cyclops problem.

I went to the inn's third floor and knocked on her door.

"It's me," I said.

"Come in."

Using the pass key, I opened the door. Sophie was lying atop her bed watching TV while sharpening a sword. How many people sharpen swords while watching *Wheel of Fortune*?

"I hope that thing's full of magic," I said. "Another monster came through the Veil."

I parked in the parking lot near the fort. Samson's truck and two patrol cars were the only vehicles there, so he must have contained the knowledge of this to only the officers first on the scene. How he would prevent them from spreading the word about a giant marauding cyclops, I had no idea.

We walked along a path toward the seventeenth-century fortress through a wide yard. The yard was designed to be a killing field for attacking infantry. The tops of the towering walls were studded with the black barrels of cannons and topped with historic flags from the Kingdom of Spain. The walls themselves were made from locally quarried coquina rock, famed for being soft enough to catch the cannon balls like a catcher's mitt instead of being shattered by them.

Low-mounted lights bathed the fortress. The light caught the head of the one-eyed giant protruding above the wall for a few moments until he wandered in the other direction.

"This is not good," I said. "The night is too young, and there are lots of tourists wandering around."

"Why are the guilds so obsessed with secrecy?" Sophie asked. "I think it's time for people to learn about the supernatural world around us."

"This is definitely *not* the time for that. With the misinformation, disinformation, and conspiracy theories all over social media and other channels, most people are more irrational than medieval peasants. Can you imagine all the false rumors spreading when people realize their neighbors could secretly be vampires, werewolves, or witches? Can you imagine how many innocent people and supernaturals would be harmed?"

"I didn't think of it that way," Sophie said. "I guess I had a higher opinion of people."

"Ah, the naivete of youth."

"And the cynicism of old people."

"Who are you calling old? Look, there's Samson by the gate. Tonight, you have one focus: sending the cyclops back to Hell or whatever you want to call what's on the other side of the Veil. He's not here to coexist with his new neighbors. He's here to eat them."

"Got it." She stopped on the path and knelt before her upright sword. "Haarg, I beseech thee to fill me with the savagery and courage of a warrior."

She rose and looked at me. "I'm ready."

Her eyes had filled with an intensity that was, frankly, scary.

"Right this way," Samson said, opening a normal-sized door built within the massive wooden and iron gate. "The monster will see you now."

This was not the regular tourist entrance that was on a higher level. This gate led to the ground-level parade ground inside the fort where an army would march in.

Tonight, the army was simply Sophie, armed with a broadsword and an ultra-potent blend of elemental and Fae magic.

On the far side of the parade ground, the twenty-foot-tall giant chased a remaining security guard. The panicked man squeezed into a narrow stone passageway just in time.

The cyclops turned and spotted us.

He was a hominid in appearance, hairy, muscular, and clad in animal skins. His face was bearded, and just above his nose was his single eye. It regarded us hungrily.

I walked in front, with Sophie behind me and Samson to our side, armed with a shotgun and his handgun, though I had little faith in them being able to stop the giant. Samson had ordered the three uniformed officers who were on the scene to keep tourists from getting near the fort.

The cyclops plodded toward us, and I began to sing. Yeah, it sounds silly, but like I said before, I couldn't kill him. I could only use my goddess powers to pacify him, hopefully enough that I could summon a gateway to whisk him away beyond the Veil.

I sang in an ancient tongue, feeling the divine energy warm my solar plexus and spread throughout my body. I sent waves of it from my fingers toward the cyclops—pure rays of love.

He wasn't buying it. His walk turned into a full-on, lumbering sprint toward us.

Samson cocked the shotgun.

"Don't shoot," Sophie said, stepping in front of me.

The human incarnation of the earth-mother goddess, having failed to win over the monster, stepped aside and let her war-witch daughter take over.

Sophie crouched. Holding the sword in two hands, she pointed it at the cyclops. The monster was crossing the distance between us much too quickly. Her lips moved as she chanted the words to a spell.

When her sword suddenly glowed purple, my fear decreased a bit.

"Stop, I command you!" Sophie bellowed.

The monster winced, his single eye closing slightly. But he didn't stop his charge.

Sophie screamed words I recognized as Fae but couldn't understand.

And blue lightning shot from the point of her sword, hitting the cyclops right in the eye.

He bellowed in pain and stumbled, falling to his knees. We

were within his reach before we backed away, just as he dove for us.

The ground shook as he landed on his stomach.

But he scrambled to his knees with a remarkable agility for a giant.

Something shot past me toward the cyclops. It was my daughter. She shouted something in Fae and leaped, plunging her sword into the monster's eye before he could stand.

He dropped like a fallen tower, Sophie dancing out of the way.

While the giant lay face-down on the ground, she blasted him with more blue lightning. He shuddered, then remained still.

"The foe is vanquished," she said in the overly dramatic way she had when under the influence of Haarg.

"How in the world are we going to get his body out of here?" Samson asked.

His answer came seconds later.

The cyclops shrank before our eyes, as if we were looking through a telephoto lens that was zooming out. Soon the giant was the size of a toy, then an insect.

Soon, he was completely gone.

"Wow, very handy," Samson said.

"We did it, Mom! We defeated him!"

"No, Sophie, you did it. I wasn't any help."

"You were. You slowed him at first and weakened his resolve, giving me time to cast my spell. I think we make a great team."

"Yes, we do."

But a team meant for what? Ridding the world of monsters from beyond the Veil?

They say sharing common interests is good for mother-daughter bonding. We shall see.

CHAPTER 8

A SPELL OF A PROBLEM

It was the closest thing I'd ever seen to a witches' sabbath. Twelve magicians—a mage, a wizard, and ten witches—stood in a circle facing inward on the beach at midnight under a full moon. Including Arch Mage Bob and Sophie, they were all water witches. They were here beside the ocean, literally in their element, combining their energies to produce the most powerful magic they could.

The thought of how they were magnifying their energies through connecting with one another and the sea gave me a twinge of sadness. Cory could draw upon the immense power of the earth by tapping into ley lines running beneath the surface. But he had stopped doing that. Texas Tom, the evil wizard, had exploited Cory to steal this energy, and Cory had given up practicing magic, suffering from PTSD.

Arch Mage Bob stood closest to the ocean, his feet in the surf's froth, his shaggy blond hair waving in the wind. Sophie held his hand, and a witch I didn't know held his other. The sand was silver in the moonlight, with the dark coquina rock formations resembling crouching beasts.

Bob chanted in a booming voice, easily heard above the low rumble of the surf. Even though his words were in Latin, Hebrew, and ancient Babylonian, he didn't lose his surfer's drawl.

I sat on a rock more than a dozen yards away yet could feel the energy building in the circle. It felt powerful and dangerous, like being outside during a lightning storm.

Earlier, Bob had told me about the spell's complexity and its very simple purpose that used what I had learned about the Father of Lies: to leverage his deep insecurity by revealing to him what he truly was—a house of cards built on lies. A false god with no actual power other than what he stole from the humans and other species he manipulated.

In short, the Father of Lies was nothing but a sham.

Once, when the fallen angel visited my cottage, I had scored a blow against him by showing him his reflection in a mirror. The spell being cast tonight was using the same tactic, though on a much grander cosmic scale.

If the demon could be wounded and weakened, Bob believed a standard negation spell would break the one that infected the vampires of San Marcos.

Thunder shook the earth, startling me. Those in the witches' circle didn't seem to notice. Lightning snaked across the sky, but it wasn't jagged like typical bolts. It flowed sinuously, like streams of molten lava.

I admit I was frightened. Bob and his witches were messing with the forces of the universe, even if in a limited area seen by us alone. They believed manipulating these forces was the only way they could harm a god-slash-demon.

Now, the entire circle of witches was chanting, repeating certain words and phrases intoned by Bob. The amount of static electricity in the air made all the hairs on my body stand on end.

My stomach ached. I felt queasy, too, like I did when the angels I still called gateways transported me to different times and planes of existence.

Thunder boomed even louder. More rivulets of lightning crossed the sky.

My breath was swept away when the entire sky turned silver. It didn't change the moonlight that illuminated the beach. But instead of a black sky with a glowing moon and stars, the heavens were a uniform chrome.

The people in the circle didn't even look up, so absorbed were they in their spell-casting.

My eyes returned to the sky. I was completely fascinated by it, and I sensed something even more dramatic would happen soon. I was right.

A face appeared in the sky, like a close-up of an actor on a drive-in movie screen. It was an elderly bearded man I recognized as the visitor to my cottage not long ago. He looked dapper and vain.

Then, his face melted until it was nothing but a skull. Seconds later, the skull dissolved into dust.

The dust rained down, stinging my exposed skin like sand whipped by a strong wind.

A demonic laughter followed. It came from every direction and startled the witches out of their concentration.

"Nice try, foolish humans," a cultured voice said in my head, and probably everyone else's. "You assumed I would respond to human psychology, but you are wrong and simple-minded, like all humans. I am an angel who became a god. Your attempt to weaken my self-confidence means nothing to me."

The sky was back to normal, and the witches released each

other's hands now that their spell had been broken. They looked lost and confused, staring at Bob for guidance. He was just as befuddled as they were.

"As punishment to you foolish humans, I will resume where the Fae left off," the voice said in my brain. "I will lead the vampires who are under my spell. And they will destroy all of you."

Bob glanced at me, his expression shattered and hopeless.

"It's a total fail, dude," he said.

No kidding.

"SO, HOW WAS YOUR SPELL-CASTING TONIGHT?" CORY ASKED cheerily when Sophie and I returned home.

"Don't ask," Sophie said.

"The spell backfired," I explained. "Instead of using the Father of Lies' insecurity to weaken him, we only made him mad. He's retaliating by sending the infected vampires after us."

"You're saying you actually made matters worse?"

"Exactly."

"What's going to happen to the elder female vampire who is trying to take over?"

"Your guess is as good as mine. The Father of Lies said he'll order the infected vampires to attack humans. Maybe that will leave them just as vulnerable as before to attack from normal vampires."

"Will that make this elder vampire your ally?"

"No. She wants nothing except power. Humans mean nothing to her. We're just food. She doesn't care if she starts a civil war between vampires that reveals their existence to the world."

"Oh." Cory frowned. "I think it would be a good time for us to move back to Key West."

"If we're entering a vampire apocalypse, we won't be safe anywhere."

As if he'd heard our conversation from across town, Diego rang the doorbell. His face was grave when I let him in.

"What is going on?" he asked. "Are the Fae attacking again? I sense disruption in the vampire community, and as I was coming here, I saw two infected vampires attack a man right in the open."

"Did they kill the man?"

"I'm afraid so."

"Did they turn him?"

"No."

"See, there's a bright side to everything."

"Please turn your sarcasm down a few notches," Cory said.

I recounted to Diego the spell-casting at the beach, how it failed, and what the Father of Lies vowed to do.

"I must confess, these are the direst straits our vampire community has ever experienced," Diego said. "I've been in San Marcos since the very beginning, not long after it was founded in fifteen sixty-five. We vampires had to hide our nature while the city was attacked by the English and by pirates repeatedly. The English burned the whole place down in fifteen eighty-six, the residents scattered into the countryside, and we vampires had to survive without being found out. We even survived the Spanish Inquisition. Since then, we worked hard to build our fortunes, and even as our numbers grew, we preyed upon humans responsibly and sustainably, so both populations were healthy."

I wanted to make a joke about free-range humans and farm-to-fang, but the look of despair in Diego's eyes stopped me.

"If the city breaks out in a slaughter," he said softly, "all will be lost."

I patted his arm beneath his expensive cashmere sport coat. He was a strikingly handsome man. Raised in Spain from African descent, he was called a Moor back in those days, though he had no connection with the Muslims who had conquered southern Spain before being driven out by Ferdinand and Isabella.

His tortured eyes met mine, and a powerful wave of empathy filled me. Maybe it was the Goddess's doing, but I'd never felt so in tune with a vampire before.

"We'll get through this," I said in a soothing voice. "In the meantime, you must be extra careful to protect yourself. Both Lethia and the infected vampires could come after you and the few local vampires who aren't infected. Oh, speak of the Devil," I said as the door opened, and Roderick came inside.

"What are you humans still doing up?" he asked. "And Diego, why did you not ask my permission before coming inside?"

"Because you weren't around, and I invited him in," I said sternly. "We have a serious problem on our hands, and we need you to cooperate. By the way, you have a drop of blood on your chin."

"Egads!" He wiped it with a handkerchief. "What is your problem?"

"It's *our* problem."

Once again, I told the story of our failed attempt to weaken the Father of Lies.

"That sounds like a rather desperate gambit."

"It sure seems so now, but at the time, we thought it would work. We didn't know of anything else we could do."

"I was under the impression that things had finally calmed

down around here now that the Fae have left. Now, I must worry about infected vampires again?"

"Yes, and also the elder who turned Mr. Jubbles."

"She and her children are greatly outnumbered by the infected vampires," Cory said. "Hopefully, they'll drive her out of town, now that they're active again."

"Never underestimate the power and cunning of an elder," Diego said.

"Not just an elder," I added. "I read her memories on the bracelet she dropped here. This is hard to believe, but she believes she is the world's first vampire, created by the Father of Lies."

Both Roderick's and Diego's mouths opened in astonishment. Thankfully, their fangs were retracted.

"That's too much of a coincidence," Cory said.

"Think about it," I said. "Existing in animated form after you've died—being undead—is a lie of sorts. No offense to my friends here."

"If what you say is true, the elder is far more powerful than I believed," said Diego. "What is more, she may turn out to be—as your husband suggested—an ally of ours in defeating the Father of Lies."

"An ally who will turn on us like a poisonous snake," Roderick said. "If she agrees to help us, she will want to rule this city."

"We'll worry about that later," I said. "Our first order of business is to make sure the infected vampires don't—"

The lights went out. Then came the scratching of nails on the outside of the doors and windows.

The inn was under attack.

CHAPTER 9

INN DANGER

"My goodness, the guests!" My throat was tight with panic. "We must protect the guests. If any return to the inn now, they'll be attacked."

"It's almost three a.m.," Cory said. "I believe they're all in their rooms."

"I hope Sophie's warding spell works against these vampires."

A window shattered in the dining room. We all hurried to the doorway to see a male vampire tangled in the thick drapes. Fangs bared, Diego charged him. In a series of moves that were acrobatic and so fast they were a blur, Diego destroyed the intruder, leaving a pile of dust at his feet.

"Nope," I said. "The warding spell didn't work."

"I'm going upstairs to get my sword," Sophie said as she sprinted for the stairs. She knew better than to take the elevator during a fire or a vampire attack.

I stepped away from the others so I could concentrate and summon the powers of the Goddess. The first time I was caught in an attack of the infected vampires, I was taken over by the

Goddess and I sang an ancient song of healing. It persuaded the vampires to retreat, but it didn't heal them.

On another occasion, when Summer and I were attacked by vampires in a state park, the Goddess gave me lethal force to eradicate the corrupted, contagious creatures. I blasted the vampires in a manner similar to how Sophie destroyed the healthy vampire in Mom's house.

I was devastated by destroying instead of healing. But, as they say, desperate times call for desperate measures. There were innocent people sleeping in this inn who needed to be protected. And, ideally, prevented from knowing we were under attack at all.

My consciousness shifted. I was no longer Darla, as the Goddess took over. The familiar warm glow in my insides turned to a burning heat that spread throughout me.

I was inside both my inn and a primeval forest at the same time. A fierce desire to protect my children—all living creatures —propelled me to action.

A vampire repeatedly threw herself at the main entrance. It was made of thick safety glass, impossible to break—or so said the company that made it. But did it come with a disclaimer excluding inhumanly strong vampires?

Each time she hit the glass with her shoulder, the door shook, and the glass appeared to flex. A normal, uninfected vampire would find smarter ways to get inside. But this feral creature could succeed only through brute force.

Power surged within me until I felt as if I would explode. Then, white light shot from my fingertips and hit the door.

The vampire flew backwards, landing on the street in a heap. She was stunned, but not destroyed. I was pleased I didn't have to destroy her.

"Heavens to Betsy! Someone's trying to break into my room!"

Mrs. Gladsen, from 204, was standing behind me in a pink muumuu, her face whiter than a vampire's because of its dense mask of facial cream.

"Through the window?" I asked.

"Yes! What is going on here?"

"Cory, take Mrs. Gladsen to the kitchen for a cup of tea."

The kitchen didn't have any windows, which I used to regret. Not anymore.

"Do you have any booze instead?" she asked.

"We do," said Cory. "Come with me."

I raced upstairs to Mrs. Gladsen's room and used the passkey card to open the door just enough that I could peer inside.

The vampire clung to the window frame with his hands and feet like a gecko, bashing the glass with his head. Did I mention the evil infection caused symptoms of acute stupidity?

Despite preserving as many of the historical details as I could in my 1736 inn, I've replaced most windows with hurricane-proof glass—this being Florida and all. The windows were specially designed to match historical design standards, but they were virtually impossible to break through. Even a feral vampire's skull couldn't do it.

My goddess state of mind had subsided only slightly, so I fired it back up. The white bolts of lightning shot from my fingers and knocked the vampire from his perch.

Looking out of the window, I saw he had fallen headfirst into a planter in the courtyard.

There were only a handful of vampires in the courtyard, milling about listlessly. I left the room and went to the window by the stairwell on the other side of the building facing Hidalgo Avenue. No vampires were visible.

I allowed myself to hope this was a minor attack that would end soon.

When I reached the ground floor, I looked through the front door. No vampires were visible. In the dining room, Sophie had her sword and was guarding the broken window. The courtyard was now empty of vampires.

The only place I hadn't checked was the side of the house facing the alley. There were no windows on the ground floor on that side, only the exterior door to the utility room.

I went down the rear hall, opened the interior door, scuffed from countless collisions with housekeeping carts, and turned on the overhead lights. The utility room is divided into a laundry area, a workshop, and storage. The exterior door to the alley had a peephole, so I went over to look.

The steel-reinforced door bulged inward as if it would burst open at any moment.

Taking a quick look through the peephole's fisheye lens, I saw a sight that nearly stopped my heart.

The alley was packed with vampires pushing toward the door, some falling beneath the surging crowd.

I stifled a scream and ran out of the room.

"They're about to break into the utility room!" I shouted, not caring if any guests heard me.

As I turned the corner into the central hallway, I met Diego and Sophie running in my direction toward the utility room.

"There's like an entire army of them in the alley. They're about to break the door down."

Cory and Roderick were still in the dining room, looking confused.

"Roderick, come with me to the utility room. We need another vampire on our side."

"Erm, I was guarding the broken window."

"Cory can do that."

Cory held a length of sharpened rebar. Ever since an infected

85

vampire abducted Sophie, and an ogre-turned-vampire broke into our cottage, he had hidden spear-like weapons throughout the property in case of emergencies like this.

"But Cory should have a vampire at his side," Roderick protested.

"Come with me now! We need to defend the utility room."

As I ran back the way I had come, hoping Roderick was following, a whine of breaking metal and a loud bang came from the utility room.

The vampires had breached the door.

When I arrived, Sophie was in front of the door, shooting purple lightning from her sword at the throng of vampires attempting to squeeze through the doorway. Their madness made them too stupid to file through the door in an orderly fashion. And they paid for it—one after another was destroyed by the magic flying from Sophie's sword.

Diego was stationed just behind her, staking the few that got past Sophie's fire with one of Cory's rebars.

I forced myself into a trance, begging the Goddess to awaken in me. Soon, I was sending my white bolts of power at the door from a different angle.

Roderick shuffled into the room. "For heaven's sake, you don't expect me to stake them, do you? That is utterly barbaric."

"There's a stake over there." Diego pointed to an alcove behind the washing machines. "Use it."

With me using the Goddess's power to cleanse disease as additional firepower, no vampires were getting into the room. They were dropping into piles of dust just outside the door.

The vampires silently surged forward to their destruction. The only sounds were their grunts and scuffling shoes as they pushed blindly forward.

"Hold your fire!" Diego shouted. "That's Pedro."

The leader of the Clan of the Eternal Night was no longer leading anyone. He fought in the scrum to get to the door, just like the vampires he once managed and led. His eyes and mouth were wide with madness, his fangs dirty from lack of care.

Sprinting past Sophie as if she wasn't there, he went straight for Diego.

His protégé froze, unable to thrust his stake into his former mentor.

I screamed when Pedro tackled Diego and his jaws went right for the throat.

Praying for the Goddess to give me guidance, I broke into song, attempting to send healing, pacifying energy into Pedro.

It wasn't working. The two vampires thrashed on the concrete floor, jaws snapping, fingernails slashing, blood spattering everywhere.

Pedro was an older, more powerful vampire than Diego. And infected with madness, he was winning this fight to the death.

"Pedro, Pedro," Diego cried, on his back with his mentor's jaws around his windpipe. "Do you not recognize me?"

Pedro raised his head, snarled, and went in for the kill.

The sharpened rebar slid easily into his back, between his ribs.

Roderick withdrew it and stabbed a second time. Pedro stiffened, then dissolved into dust.

Roderick met my gaze, his eyes full of horror from what he had done.

"You saved Diego," I said to him. "Thank you."

The grunting and the scuffling in the doorway continued, and we had to return our attention to destroying vampires. Before I did so, I glanced back at Roderick. He stood in the same position, staring down at the pile of dust that used to be Pedro. His shoulders heaved as he fought his sobs.

I reoriented myself to the Goddess, returning to my semi-trance state. But there was a disturbance out in the alleyway. The vampires stopped attacking and moved aside for the individual who was pushing through them to reach the door.

It was a woman vampire, her eyes clear and steady. She was clearly not infected. She parted the vampires like the Red Sea and reached the doorway.

Though I'd only seen her through the window once, I knew her best from her memories. It was the elder vampire, Lethia.

The world's first vampire.

CHAPTER 10

VAMPIRE IN YOGA PANTS

Lethia appeared to be in her late twenties in body age. She had a giant mane of red hair in the latest style (unlike mine, which was just allowed to hang). She wore tight-fitting gray yoga pants (don't all vampires?) and a white top that revealed a well-toned midriff. Heavy makeup disguised her undead pallor. The lip gloss was the crimson of blood. Her green eyes sparkled with intelligence.

The powerful elder successfully penetrated Bob's warding spell when she attacked Mr. Jubbles and did so again with Sophie's spell, to allow the infected vampires in.

She studied me and my companions.

Suddenly, Sophie shot her with the purple lightning.

It had no effect on the elder. She didn't even flinch. Sophie tried again with the same result.

"That was rude," the vampire said.

"Sorry," I replied. "We were fighting for our lives until you walked in. Can I help you? I'm afraid we're all booked at the moment."

"My name is Lethia," the elder said, while the vampires behind her shifted their feet with impatience and growled.

"I know."

She smirked. "Yes, you have the paranormal in you along with the supernatural presence of the Goddess Danu. And your human name is?"

"Darla Chesswick. Do you have business with me?"

Lethia looked surprised, then smirked again.

"I do, but I'm rather busy right now. I was given an assignment by my maker—to lead these brain-dead vampires to wipe out the supernatural guilds of San Marcos. This is our first stop."

"You want to rule the vampires here, though, don't you?" I asked, taking the risk of being too forward.

"Not in this way. I want to do it on my own terms."

She glanced at Roderick and Diego, her eyes lingering on the latter.

"You two are not infected?"

They shook their heads.

"Whom do you follow?"

"I follow no one," Roderick said pompously. "I'm not even a member of the guild."

"I followed Pedro," Diego said with sadness, looking down at the pile of dust. "Until the madness took him over."

"You can follow me," said Lethia.

"Not while you are working for the Father of Lies. The Clan of the Eternal Night was independent and proud. I want to return to those days."

"Perhaps you will. You," she turned suddenly back to me, "have something of mine I misplaced."

I acted confused. "No. I don't know what you're talking about."

"A bracelet I lost. You must have it—how else would you know about me with your paranormal ability?"

"I learned about you from objects you touched in a house where you slaughtered a nest of vampires."

"They were infected," she said, dismissing the gravity of what she'd done. "You've slaughtered more vampires tonight than the ones in the house."

"Because they're trying to kill us."

Lethia stepped further into the room.

"Are you the vampire who lives here?" she asked Roderick.

He nodded.

"I request permission to enter." She said it as a demand, not a request.

He nodded, running his finger beneath his dress-shirt collar, as if it were too tight.

She didn't ask my permission, and I am the owner.

She passed through the interior door of the utility room with me right behind her. The layout of the ground floor was obviously familiar to her as she made it to the supply closet across from the kitchen.

Cory stepped from the dining room to see who was walking around.

"I am looking for something I lost," she told him. Pointing to the sharpened rebar he held, she added, "You won't need that."

The closet was locked, but she possessed magic of some sort that unlocked it without a pause. She bent over and searched the closet floor, not finding anything, of course.

"I believe you have my bracelet," she said to me.

"I'm sorry, but I don't," I lied.

"Normally, I would torture you to get the truth. But I don't have time for that now. You and I have other matters to discuss. I hope you will return the bracelet to me then. I sense it is here."

"I promise I will look for it and ask the staff. But I have a question for you. Why did you send the vampires here to attack us if you were commanded to destroy the guilds?"

"The Father of Lies sent them here because you and your daughter attempted to use magic against him. Now that he made me his general, I shall spare you and your daughter. For now."

She left so quickly her movements were a blur.

"That is one powerful vampire," Cory said. "I don't practice magic anymore, but I'm still sensitive to supernatural powers. You don't want to get on her bad side."

"I wish I knew what she wants from me, aside from the bracelet. I'm sure it's not going to be good for me."

I wondered what kind of power the bracelet allegedly held. Lethia clearly lusted for power. Did she plan to steal from me the Goddess's power?

Cory followed me back to the utility room. Sophie still guarded the broken exterior door, although the feral vampires were nowhere to be seen, except for piles of dust from those who had been destroyed.

Diego knelt before the pile that had once been Pedro. Roderick stood to the side, as much in shock as a vampire could exhibit.

"Why didn't she kill us?" Sophie asked.

"She has other plans for us. What they are, I don't know."

"I can't believe I couldn't destroy her."

"She's the oldest vampire on earth. Or so she believes. Would that make her the most powerful?"

Diego nodded.

"How do you defeat the world's most powerful vampire?" Sophie asked.

"You can't."

"I don't believe that. No creature or entity is all-powerful except for God himself. Even the other gods, the ones from pantheistic cultures, can be forgotten by humans, and with no one to worship them, they fade away."

"Is Lethia a goddess?" I asked Diego.

"Of course not. But she can't be defeated by humans or other vampires—I'll leave it at that."

"Speaking of gods," Sophie said, "I invited Haarg to dinner, Mom, to meet you and Cory."

"Now, of all times?"

"I'll help you with hosting. You won't even have to cook—I'll have it catered."

"What kinds of foods does a Fae god eat?"

"Being the God of War, he's definitely not a vegetarian."

DIEGO WAS THE LAST TO LEAVE THAT NIGHT. I RETURNED TO the utility room before going to bed and found him once again kneeling beside the pile of dust that had been Pedro. A single tear rolled slowly down his cheek. It was the color of blood.

He looked up when I entered, struggling to contain his emotions.

"I'm very sorry for your loss," I said, placing my hand on his shoulder. "I wish I could say something more eloquent, but I feel so empty."

"He was good to me as my maker," Diego said softly, returning his gaze to Pedro's clothing amid the dust. "In those early days, it was dangerous for vampires in San Marcos. He taught me many tricks of survival. We became close friends and stayed close through the centuries."

"Please don't blame Roderick."

"Of course, I don't. Roderick saved me. I blame Aastacki for infecting Pedro with this cursed spell. It makes me even more determined to stop that demon."

He put a hand on top of mine, and a jolt of energy passed through me. It wasn't from any sort of magic other than the simple magic of his sex appeal.

This was a totally inappropriate time for me to fall under his spell. Not only because of the tragedy that happened here, but because I'm in love with Cory.

"Your hand is so cold," I said without thinking. "I've never gotten used to a vampire's touch."

Diego turned his head and caught my eyes. His dark skin and sharp, European features made him exotically handsome.

Out of nowhere came a powerful urge to kiss him. I fought it with every ounce of strength I had.

"Humans easily become accustomed to a vampire's touch," he said.

I remembered he was in a relationship with Pedro's human housekeeper.

"The question is," he continued, "could a vampire ever get used to a Goddess's touch?"

He stood, and I withdrew my hand, stepping backwards out of the temptation zone.

"I'm more human than Goddess," I said. "I'm still mortal as far as I know."

"That is best. Your husband is mortal. And no one wants to go through eternity missing a loved one who was lost. As you can see from my dear friend, Pedro, even immortals can be taken from us."

I thought about Lethia and her desire to end her existence. It made me feel even sadder.

"Be strong, Diego. We need you. And we'll be here for you for as long as we mortals can.

"THIS EMERGENCY MEETING OF THE EXECUTIVE COUNCIL WILL now come to order," Dr. Noordlun said.

"Dude, it's like every council meeting now is an emergency meeting," Arch Mage Bob said.

Everyone else grumbled in agreement.

"Please restate to the council what you reported," Dr. Noordlun requested of me.

"After the Magic Guild's attempt to weaken the Father of Lies failed, he vowed he'd get revenge by sending the infected vampires to attack us. He wants to wipe out all the guilds."

Murmurs of disbelief and dismay echoed throughout the meeting room.

"And the vampire we last discussed, Lethia, was appointed to be commander of the vampires."

"He gave her what she wanted," Baldric said. "She was going to wipe out the infected vampires, and now they belong to her."

"She got what she wanted, but she's still subservient to the Father of Lies. I doubt she enjoys that."

"This makes it even more imperative that we get rid of her," Rufus said.

"You can't destroy her," Diego said once again.

"There must be something we can do," Dr. Noordlun said. "Bob, do you have magic that will drive her away?"

"The warding spells I've used against the Fae and the infected vampires didn't work on her. If she's, like, that powerful, will any magic at all work against her?"

"If Cory harvested energy from the ley lines, would that help?" I would hate to put Cory through that trauma again, but we were desperate.

"The energy we made for the spell against the Father of Lies was just as strong, and still, it wasn't enough."

"Not enough for him, but maybe enough to drive away Lethia."

Bob frowned, unconvinced.

I got an idea. "Her bracelet—her memories said it had a special power. Can you examine it? Maybe it can help us."

"I'll try. Bring it by the surf shop."

"Okay. During daylight hours. I can't risk carrying it around at night because she's looking for it. If we can't harvest its power, my cousin Missy has a locator spell that can use the bracelet to find Lethia."

"Missy Mindle? Yeah, she has the best locator spell I know of."

Coming from an Arch Mage, that was a genuine compliment.

"If we find Lethia, we need to stake her," Rufus said. He glanced at Diego. "Even if she's too powerful, we must at least try to destroy her."

The other members of the council agreed.

YEAH, HAARG LOOKED LIKE A GOD. I MEAN, HE WASN'T AS attractive as Sophie had led me to believe, but he was handsome, nevertheless. The best word to describe him was formidable. He was tall and muscular, but the muscles looked hard and effective —not a pumped-up bodybuilder physique. His black hair was cut military style. His jaw was square, and his eyes were piercing in a slightly scary way.

Because he was a Fae god, I assumed his incarnated form was small, with oddly proportioned facial features, as was the case with faeries. Not so. This must be only the form he took on when with humans, as the Fae often do.

Cory winced when they shook hands. Be careful with a war god, I should have told him.

We began by sipping human wines, making small talk about the weather, the abundance of tourists in San Marcos this season, and the psychological benefits of burning your enemies' villages to the ground.

It got a little awkward when Sophie served hors d'oeuvres. The Fae consider steamed lizards to be a delicacy—the little anoles and geckos we have in Florida—and Cory's face went pale as he watched Haarg snack lustily upon them. Honestly, if you're okay watching people at a crawfish boil, you'd have no problem with Haarg's snacking.

Sophie had procured a meal of roasted wild boar and parsnips, which delighted Haarg, but was a bit gamey for my tastes.

As a mother, I was most intent on observing the chemistry between the war god and my daughter. It was just short of a nuclear reaction.

It wasn't until the dessert of raw honeycombs that the topic of gods and goddesses came up.

"So, Mrs. Chesswick—"

"You can call me Darla."

"Thank you, Darla, Daughter of Danu. I do not understand if you are mortal or immortal?"

"I am a mortal human who has taken on the responsibility of being the living representative of the goddess. Let me ask you, are you the same as other gods of war, such as Mars and Odin?"

"No relation at all. If you are human, then are you really Danu's priestess?"

"No. The Goddess exists inside me. In terms of my mortality,

I don't know if she has changed my physiology. I noticed a new gray hair yesterday, so I guess I'm still mortal."

"You look as beautiful as the day we married," Cory said.

Haarg frowned at him. War gods are not much for sentimentality.

"Can you slay anyone with your powers?" he asked me.

"My powers are for healing and engendering. I am a mother goddess, fostering life upon this earth."

"Bor-ing."

"I have slain an invasive root mold and a few infected vampires because they are harmful to healthy creatures. Now, you tell me, Haarg, can you slay another god?"

"Another god? That is simply not common, though we might battle from time to time."

"I'm asking because of Aastacki. He has become a major problem. We humans call him the Father of Lies. Do you know him well?"

Haarg fiddled with his fork. "No, not anymore."

"We need to break a spell he has created. Is there any way you can help us?"

"We gods don't like to interfere with the affairs of humans."

"Except when you do. Which is all the time."

"Mom," Sophie pleaded with me.

"Sophie's life has been put in danger because of Aastacki."

Haarg turned to Sophie. "Is this true?"

"Well, indirectly, yes."

Haarg slammed his fist on the table, sending the plates and silverware jumping.

"I will deal with this scoundrel. In every pantheon of gods, there is a trickster like him, and I have no respect for them. If needed, I will fight him, one on one."

"We don't want to inconvenience you," Cory said.

"Go for it," I said. "It can be like Joe Frazier versus Muhammad Ali."

"And if I win, I shall ask for the hand of your daughter."

Silence.

Sophie beamed at Haarg. Cory awkwardly cut a piece of honeycomb with his dessert fork. I had to say something.

"Thank you for asking. If this is what Sophie wants, I approve."

Cory smiled weakly at Haarg and nodded. The god kissed my daughter.

"How exactly did a mortal attract the attention of a god?" Cory ruined the mood. "Just asking."

"The Fae magic I was being taught invoked the power of Haarg," Sophie explained.

"And I noticed she was hot," Haarg said. "Aside from Aphrodite, there just aren't many hot goddesses. I mean, except for you, Mrs. Chesswick. So, if you want hot chicks, you have to go for mortals."

"I see," Cory said with a frown.

At least he's not some loser with an arrest record, I told myself.

CHAPTER 11

FEEL THE MAGIC

It was late morning, the dazzling sun glinting off the smooth surface of the Atlantic Ocean. A V-shaped formation of pelicans flew low over the white sand parallel to the water's edge.

Ostensibly, it was a safe time to be outside if you wanted to avoid vampires. That didn't quell my nervousness as I drove along Highway A1A to Pagan Surf Shop with the snake bracelet.

The store was usually busy with tourists shopping for bathing suits and sunglasses. Today, with a flat sea, surfers were here, too, looking to upgrade their boards or just hanging out. I found Bob alone in his office next to his board workshop.

"It's hard to think of magic on a beautiful day like this," I said as he rolled himself in his desk chair to me and gave me a fist bump.

"No way. Magic is everywhere all the time, especially when nature is showing off."

"Here's the bracelet," I said, removing it from the white plastic evidence bag it was in when Samson returned it.

"Whoa, this is so old. It's like a museum piece. This has got to be worth a fortune."

"It's important to Lethia, I assume because of more than sentimental value."

He held it in his big, calloused hand. "I feel the magic."

"I felt it, too. But I don't have the training to identify the magic. Neither does Sophie. We need a mage like you."

"There's more than one layer of magic in it," Bob said. "Added at different times. Maybe hundreds of years apart. You say this is a very old vampire?"

"Allegedly, the very first."

Bob placed his other hand atop the one that held the bracelet. He closed his eyes and was silent for an awkwardly long period.

"One spell I can identify is a glamour spell. She probably used it to help her mesmerize victims. As the first vampire, she probably had to develop the ability to mesmerize."

"The Father of Lies must have cast it for her when he made her a vampire. She bought the bracelet from its artisan in adulthood, probably not long before she died and was brought back."

"There are more layers of magic than I realized," Bob said, his eyes still closed. "Minor charms and spells. But there's something else, like, way more powerful, added much later. Can't tell what it is. And though it's powerful, there are only traces of it on the bracelet. I think the core of the power is inside of her."

He was silent for a long time, his palms still sandwiching the bracelet.

He opened his eyes. "I need to use a spell to identify it."

"I hope the Father of Lies has nothing to do with it. We don't need more problems from him."

Bob frowned. "For sure."

He placed the bracelet on his desk and walked to the corner

of the workshop, opening a tall cabinet next to a rack where freshly epoxied surfboards were drying. He withdrew a wooden staff, still shaped like the branch it had once been, but worn smooth by years of handling.

"A staff? I didn't know you used one."

"It's from my wizard days. She's been with me through some gnarly stuff and never let me down. I still use her from time to time since becoming a mage. Helps me focus my magic when I'm feeling my way through a problem. Kind of like using your trusty long board to get a feel for weird surf patterns."

"Of course," I said, though I had no idea what he meant.

He held the staff casually in one hand as he brought it to the desk. But when he grasped it with his other hand, I immediately felt the crackle of energy in the air.

"Wow," I said.

"Yup. She's still got it."

He closed his eyes and held the staff horizontally with his arms extended. I could swear the staff glowed, but it could be my imagination.

A few strands of Bob's shaggy hair stood on end. My scalp tingled as my hair did the same.

In one fluid motion, Bob swung the staff gently downwards until it touched the bracelet. A flash of light, followed by a loud pop came from where the wood touched the metal.

Suddenly, I became dizzy. My stomach burned. The fire spread throughout me, and I felt as if I would explode.

Bob lifted the staff from the bracelet, and I felt perfectly normal again.

"That was weird," I said.

"Totally. The power in the bracelet isn't a magic spell. It's divine power—like from a god. I don't know what it does, though. Sorry."

"I felt burning inside of me. Was it Danu reacting because it's a divine power?"

"I don't know. But that's a good enough guess. The problem is you weren't the only one affected by it."

"What do you mean?"

"When my staff connected with the power, it caused a brief disruption in the magic field. I felt eyes staring at me. Someone was alerted by the disruption."

"Someone like Lethia?"

"Could be." He looked out the window, nervous, as if the vampire would be out in the bright sunshine. "If so, she had a strong connection with the bracelet and its power. She really wants it back."

That meant Lethia would eventually figure out I have it and would pay me a visit again. I might not survive the visit.

It was critical to find her first, to destroy her somehow, or at least drive her from San Marcos before the vampires wiped us all out.

I explained to Bob the severity of the crisis.

"If Sophie's magic didn't destroy Lethia, what are you going to do?"

"I don't know. I tend to figure things out as I go along."

"Sounds risky to me."

"Don't I know it?"

JUST AFTER DAWN THE FOLLOWING MORNING, BOB CALLED ME.

"Someone paid a visit to my shop last night. Somehow, the alarm system was disabled. My warding spell was breached, too. It warned me it was breached, but I wasn't going to go to the shop and check on it before sunrise."

"It must have been her, since she got through the warding spell before," I said. "Unless humans can get through the spell."

"The spell is for vampires and other undead creatures. That's why it warned me."

"Did she damage anything?"

"No. She must have realized right away that the bracelet wasn't here. I guess she went to the location where my staff touched the power in the bracelet."

That was good to know. It meant she wouldn't be able to find it right away at the inn. However, she surely suspects I have it.

"Be very careful," Bob said, as if reading my thoughts.

"Missy, you look great!" I said, giving my much taller cousin a big hug.

"So do you."

"I'm sure the stress shows in my face."

"Does it have to do with the vampire you want me to find?"

"Yes. I've got a heap of vampire troubles."

"They can be a pain in the neck. No pun intended."

"Right. Lots of your home health patients are vampires."

"Cantankerous old vampires."

"You know vampires better than anyone. I need to get rid of one. She's young in body age, but positively ancient in true age. She believes she was the world's first vampire."

"Oh, my. I think this is out of my league."

"You're all I've got, Missy."

Missy joined my guests for the afternoon tea service, but I was too busy serving them to chat with her. It wasn't until dinner that we had the leisure to catch up.

Since Missy was so down to earth, she didn't mind eating in

our tiny cottage dining alcove. Cory was there, of course, and I made sure Sophie joined us. I wanted to give the witches the chance to talk shop.

"Thanks for casting a warding spell," I said to Missy as I passed her the platter of locally caught flounder. "Bob's spell simply wasn't up to the task. Sophie's spell was breached, too."

"I can't guarantee mine will do any better than theirs. And Bob's a mage, after all."

"Does that really matter?" Sophie asked. "Isn't it all about the spell itself, not who cast it?"

"If cast correctly, a certain spell will function the same regardless of who cast it. But—and this is a big but—a more powerful magician can add extra oomph to the spell."

"I hope you gave it enough oomph to keep Lethia away," I said.

"I tried. And I'm sure my spell was different from the ones you guys used. I deal with a lot of vampires. My warding spell is specifically designed for them."

"I need to learn a better warding spell," Sophie said glumly.

"What kind of magic do you prefer?"

"At first, it was elemental magic, because I'm a water witch. Then, I received training from a faerie. He taught me battle magic. I guess I prefer attack spells over defensive ones."

"Especially since your 'friend' is the Fae war god," Cory said.

"Oh, my. Your side of the family has so much involvement with deities," said Missy.

"We didn't seek it out," I added.

"My apologies for mentioning this, but you need to be careful with battle magic," Missy said to Sophie. "Look no further than my mother—your aunt—for the reason why."

"I don't practice black magic. I never will."

"Sometimes, it's hard to tell when you cross the line into black magic."

"I attack monsters only," Sophie said defensively.

"She's quite good at it," I said. "Vampires, anthropophagi. . ."

"Anthro-*what?*"

"Legendary monsters from the ancient world. They're humanoid, but don't have heads. Their mouths and eyes are on their torsos. They love to eat humans, but if you give Sophie a sword, they don't stand a chance against her. They're just some of the legendary monsters that have come through the tear in the Veil."

Missy stared at me, a bite of fish perched on her fork.

"I told you about the problem with the Veil," I reminded her.

"You mentioned it once or twice in passing when chatting on the phone. I thought it was more of a metaphor."

"Darla enjoys downplaying the danger she gets into," Cory said. "She's had a unicorn try to impale her in a supermarket and a minotaur attack her in a parking garage. A Gorgon, like Medusa, showed up here once and turned a guest to stone."

"Oh, my."

"And I had to destroy a cyclops," Sophie added.

"Oh, my."

"Yep," I said. "We have lots of fun around here."

I didn't mention the other legendary creatures I've had coming after me, such as the Questing Beast and the camazotz.

"The good news is the faerie who directed the monsters to kill me has been put out of action."

"Now, the monsters come to kill just about anyone," Sophie said.

"Oh, my."

"It's a big problem," Cory said. "This town depends on tourism, but monsters can come through the Veil at any moment. That's not even including the infected vampires and this elder vampire who wants to take over the town."

"You need to tackle monster problems one step at a time," I said. "Missy will help us find Lethia, then we can hopefully cross her off the list."

"'Cross her off the list,'" Sophie said, snickering. "You mean 'destroy her with maximum prejudice.'"

"Yep. Just trying to keep the conversation suitable for dinner."

I noticed Missy still had eaten nothing.

"Missy, relax, have some wine, and enjoy your food. I won't ask you to do your locator spell until tomorrow when we know Lethia will be sleeping. And you don't have to join us when we, um, take care of her."

Sophie gave a sinister grin. She was still perturbed that Lethia was impervious to her "battle magic."

Missy drained her glass of wine. Cory quickly refilled it.

"I didn't know things were so dangerous here," Missy said.

"Welcome to my world," I muttered.

"It's your world, but we all have to deal with it," Cory said with a touch of bitterness.

There are certain professions that put a lot of strain on marriages. Innkeeper is not supposed to be on the list. Unless the innkeeper is me.

"Mom, can I be part of the staking party tomorrow?" Sophie asked.

I put my head in my hands. So much for light dinner conversation.

The fact is, the Executive Council decided Lethia would be dealt with in the old-school manner. Because our magic didn't seem to work against her, we would resort to brute force when we found her sleeping. Yes, Diego said an elder was extremely difficult to destroy—and you didn't get any vampires older than Lethia. But we didn't know what else to do.

Cory went to fill Missy's glass again, but she used her magic to send it floating high above the table.

"I've had enough, thank you. And I'm perfectly capable of going along with you tomorrow. I brought several vampire-repellant charms and amulets with me just in case she wakes up."

The thought of Lethia fighting back before we could stake her curdled my stomach.

"Does your sleeping spell work on vampires?" I asked.

Missy nodded. "And I have an immobility spell, too."

Maybe it would be best to have Missy with us tomorrow, after all. Bob was going to be there with his magic, but Missy was such an expert on vampires.

"Okay, Missy, you can come with us, but please be careful and stay in the rear. I didn't invite you up here to put your safety in danger."

"Welcome to your world," Cory snarked at me.

CHAPTER 12

HIGH STAKES

Iretrieved the snake bracelet from the locked desk drawer in the cottage and brought it to Missy, who was drawing a magic circle on my living room floor. We had to use my cottage for the spell-casting, because it was daytime, and guests were free to wander about the inn.

I had a strange feeling holding the bracelet in my hand. I had walled myself off from reading memories during the simple task of bringing the bracelet to Missy, to prevent accidentally falling into a reverie.

Now that I was holding it normally, the bracelet was connecting with me somehow—a feeling of familiarity.

How could this be? I'd never seen it prior to finding it on the floor of the closet beside the exsanguinated body of Mr. Jubbles. No, there was something about the psychic energy the bracelet held.

I couldn't figure out what it was, so I handed it to Missy. After the handoff, she completed drawing the circle, sealing herself inside, and lit five tea candles that marked the five points of a pentagram and represented the elements of earth, water, air, fire, and spirit.

"Is it okay if I watch?" I asked.

She nodded but held a finger to her lips for silence. That's a gesture I've gotten from a lot of people over the years.

She held a match to a small copper bowl and ignited strange-smelling incense. There were peppery, herbal scents, but also something else slightly foul.

Closing her eyes, she chanted in a low tone. The words were in a language unfamiliar to me. Suddenly, I felt the crackle of magic in the room.

The magical energy intensified. I found it difficult to breathe, but not in a scary way. I sat on the couch and watched Missy build the spell, totally immersed in her ritual.

Was I imagining it, or was that a white orb floating above the bracelet on Missy's palm?

Yes, it was an orb. It grew from the size of a marble to a tennis ball, its illuminance intensifying as it hovered above the bracelet just in front of Missy's face.

"Go forth and find the spirit from which you came," Missy said.

The orb flew across the room and disappeared through the wall.

I was so tempted to open my fat mouth, but I knew better. I silently watched as Missy knelt perfectly still, her head cocked to one side.

Nothing happened for several minutes. Then, Missy nodded slightly and tilted her head back, her eyes still closed. She remained that way for a couple more minutes before opening her eyes and turning her head toward me.

"The orb you saw is a manifestation of the vampire's psychic energy she left on the bracelet," Missy said. "It's from the same energy you read for memories. I concentrated it and detached it from the bracelet. Psychic energy like that wants to rejoin its source—almost a magnetic attraction. While it searched for its source, I could see from its perspective. It traveled to a home in a neighborhood near your inn."

She described a cobblestone street, massive live oaks in front lawns, and homes from the eighteen hundreds.

"I forced the orb to float outside the house, and I noted nearby landmarks. If you can get a satellite map of this part of town, I think I can find the house."

Missy erased a section of chalk, breaking the magic circle and her spell. She rose, stiffly, from the floor.

I pulled up a map on my laptop and handed it to her. She zoomed in and out, moved the map around, then smiled.

"Here it is." She pointed to a roof with a chimney and a yard obscured by an oak.

It was the same block as the Gothic revival home where Lethia had massacred the nest of vampires.

Missy switched to street view, and I studied the two-story brick home from around the Civil War era.

"What do we do now?" she asked.

"We go in with stakes."

The team the Executive Council had assigned was Dr. Noordlun, Arch Mage Bob, a female troll named Felicia—who would easily pass for a super-muscular human—and Rufus, the Alpha of the Shifter Guild. Two additional shifters dressed as bikers rounded out the team. Missy and I were allowed to come along solely out of courtesy. We all arrived in three cars in different spots along the block.

Rufus was dressed in jogging clothes and ran down the block. He passed my car, where Missy and I sat, as casually as if he jogged this route every day.

Soon, his voice came over the handheld radio he had given us.

"I smell two humans in the house. I'm pretty sure they're guards. Arch Mage Bob, we need you to cast a sleeping spell."

Bob strolled past our car in his T-shirt, board shorts, and sandals, looking like a harmless surfer dude. He stopped in front of the target house and pretended to study his phone.

"The sleeping spell is cast," he said over the radio. "And I just unlocked the front and back doors with spells."

Gradually, the members of the team walked calmly to the house. Half went into the front door carrying tarps and painting supplies in case neighbors were watching. The others went around the sides of the house to the back. I saw various duffle bags that held the stakes.

"Okay," I said to Missy. "Let's go in."

The radio crackled. "I've counted five vampires so far, in closets and under beds. One room with closed shutters has a vampire on the bed. Not sure if there are more."

"We're only to stake the elder," Dr. Noordlun's voice said. "The one with red hair."

"Haven't seen her yet."

"Checking the attic," Rufus said.

"Be careful," the first voice said. "Bring Felicia with you."

Missy and I reached the house and went in the front door. Two humans sat slumped in the living room, passed out from the sleeping spell. All the thumping across the ceiling said everyone was upstairs.

"There's a large crate in the attic," said Rufus over the radio. "Someone get me a crowbar."

Missy and I exchanged glances.

The front door opened, and Sophie came in.

"Lethia is not here," she said.

"They're up in the attic opening a crate they believe holds her," I said.

Sophie shook her head. "No, she's not here. I sense other vampires, but not her."

"Since when have you been able to sense vampires?"

"When I identify an enemy, I become one with them. It's a skill Haarg taught me to make me a better warrior. You know the saying, know thy enemy? This takes it much further, thanks to magic."

"Then you didn't need me to cast the locator spell?" Missy asked.

"No, I needed it. I can't just find my enemy wherever they are," Sophie explained. "I need to be in their territory. The magic works with their psychic energy, I guess, like your spell."

"So, you're convinced she's not here?" I asked. "But Missy's spell located her here."

"This is her nest. She was here today only moments before you arrived. But her power as an elder must have given her the ability to escape, even though it's daytime."

"And she didn't go to the In Between," I said. "As I understand it, gateways usually won't transport vampires."

Footsteps pounded down the stairs.

"The crate is empty," Dr. Noordlun said.

"See, you should have allowed me to come along," said Sophie. "I could have saved you a lot of time and trouble. Can we destroy the other vampires?"

"No." The professor's patience had worn thin. "They've done nothing wrong."

As the team filed out of the house, frustration on each face, Sophie lingered, walking through the house.

"She's going to come for you, Mom. I just know it."

"Yeah, I guess it's inevitable. She's wanted something from

me all along. Not just the bracelet, but something greater. All the lies and warding spells in the world won't keep her away."

"Oh, my," Missy said.

"Missy, I truly appreciate your traveling up here, but I don't think it's safe for you to stay."

"I'm not abandoning you now."

"You and Cory should sleep somewhere else tonight," I said to Sophie as we left the nest house.

"Not gonna happen, Mom."

"I'll cast an additional warding spell," said Missy.

"Thank you, but no. I need to learn what she's after. If she wants to kill me, she would have done it already."

"She wants the bracelet, and then she'll kill you."

"Sophie!" Missy chided.

"She needs more than the bracelet," I said. "She has a request or questions for me. I read it in her memories."

"What are you going to tell Cory?" Sophie asked. "He won't be happy about this."

"I'll tell him I have no choice—it's my duty as the earthly manifestation of the Goddess."

"Mom, how did you end up a complete slave to your responsibilities? First the inn, then the Memory Guild, and now the Goddess?"

"I'm not a slave. My duties and I are like partners. They give me strength by serving them."

Sophie shook her head. She was not convinced.

Have you ever experienced the frustration of waiting for a guest to arrive when you don't know when it will be? My guest was one I needed to be prepared for, so I've been on edge ever since the sun faded from the horizon and my life horizon appeared to be in jeopardy of drastic shortening.

Missy and Sophie waited with me in the kitchen because it didn't have windows for a bloodsucking fiend to burst through. Roderick sat with us for a while until hunger overcame him and he went out hunting for a domestic animal.

Cory was not happy, not at all.

"Why, once again, are we in danger because of you?"

I felt as if I'd been slapped in the face.

"It's something to do with Danu, not me."

"Did Danu force you to hang onto the bracelet?"

"Um, I guess not." I allowed that he might have a point.

He sighed with exasperation and continued pacing back and forth, in and out of the kitchen. After a couple of hours, I'd had enough of it.

"Cory, why don't you get some sleep? You can get up early and stand sentinel until dawn."

He agreed with reluctance and walked from the inn to our cottage.

We three humans in the kitchen were heavily caffeinated—Sophie and I from coffee and Missy from tea. Too much caffeine, and the threat of a monster bursting in at any moment, was not a good combination.

Every strange noise caused us to jump. The fluttering of palm fronds against a window. The knocking of pipes, the slight groans as my 300-year-old structure settled—all of this was enough to drive us crazy.

To make the mood even worse, the antique grandfather clock in the foyer ticked loudly and ominously. Each click was like a nail driven into a coffin.

"We've been sitting here for hours, and still haven't agreed on a plan," Missy said.

"Yes, we have," I replied. "We're all wearing your vampire-repellant charms. If she attacks, try a sleep or immobility spell against her. Otherwise, we hear what she has to say."

"I don't know if my spells will work against her."

"They won't," Sophie said. "My plan is to ambush her when she's not looking and behead her with my sword."

"You'll do no such thing," I said, annoyed. "This is a place of hospitality and hope. We don't lop off our visitors' heads. Except as a last resort."

Sophie huffed, and I exited the room. The coffee was affecting more than my nerves, forcing yet another trip to the bathroom.

As I sat in the Victorian-styled half bath off the foyer—when I was at my most vulnerable—was when Lethia appeared right in front of me. The effect was like a ghost solidifying out of nothing.

"Do you mind?" I asked.

"I wanted to speak with you alone. If you cooperate, I will not hurt you."

"How did you simply appear in my inn like that? I didn't realize vampires have that ability."

"I do. Few other vampires can."

"Do you mind if I make myself presentable?"

"Go right ahead. But you will not escape from this room."

Vampires have little sympathy for humans' biological needs, especially since they pee only once every couple of days. She looked at me without interest, like a dog owner walking her mutt.

"I will give you your bracelet back," I said. "I didn't know for sure it was yours, and I wanted to learn as much as I could from it."

"With your psychic powers, yes?"

I nodded.

"What did you learn?"

I gave a brief summary of my findings.

"You have seen a mere glimpse of my life and undead existence. What you need to understand is this: I am compelled by magic to always be in possession of the bracelet. I will get it back no matter what it takes."

"What's so special about it? I sensed great power in it but couldn't figure out exactly what it was for."

"Aastacki, whom you call The Father of Lies, imbued it with a power that made my mesmerizing much more effective. But there is one other thing."

Her eyes softened from their cold, predatory look.

"Danu added additional, much more powerful, magic to the bracelet. You—the earth-mother goddess you represent—took pity on me and gave the bracelet the power of hope."

"Hope?" I wondered why a vampire needed hope.

"Doomed to exist for eternity, alone, with no hope of ever enjoying the rest of permanent death, I need hope to get by. To not go insane, or destroy myself willfully, through sun-scorching or another method."

"Okay. I'm glad Danu had mercy on you."

"At the time, it seemed merciful. I got through the loneliness and the curse of a never-ending existence. But now it only feels cruel to me."

"What do you mean?"

"I want you, as the representative of Danu, to end this hope magic."

"But why?"

"After thousands of years on this earth, I am ready to die. To die for once and forever."

CHAPTER 13
THE VAMPIRE'S WISH

I didn't know what to say. I had assumed Lethia had malevolent intentions toward me. Never would I have guessed that she wanted me to free her from the blessing of hope so that she could destroy herself.

I once believed that vampires, having died and returned from death by becoming vampires, would cherish their new, undead existence. So many humans sacrifice their own lives because of depression and despair. I admit, I believe some might regret their decision when they saw what death actually is.

Vampires, given a second chance at existence, would cherish it. Or so I had believed.

Finding the key to immortality was a longing that humans have always had. But apparently, the price a vampire must pay for it was too steep for Lethia.

"Why would you want to end your existence?" I asked. No, this was not the way to speak to someone in despair, but Lethia wasn't a someone. She was a vampire standing inches away from me in my half-bath after mysteriously materializing while I was doing my business.

"It has gone on much too long," she replied. "I am bored, jaded, lonely, and tired of this world. I have seen too much and want to forget it all."

"But the alternative is worse."

"In the bleak nothingness of non-existence, at least there are no politicians."

"Okay. Point taken. But seriously, do you know what non-existence is like? Have you been beyond the Veil?"

"I have not, but I understand exactly what non-existence is."

"May I ask why you feel lonely?"

Lethia looked at me as if it was the dumbest question she'd heard in her millennia on earth.

"I mean, you've already created several children here in San Marcos," I added.

She turned away from me, her head against the wall, her hands resting on the towel bar.

"They're not true children," she said. "They're followers who beg me to teach them how to be vampires."

"Why did you create them?"

"Because I need to." Her shoulders tensed.

"I've also been wondering how many followers you have in other cities. After all these centuries, you must have so many."

An explosive *crack* reverberated in the tiny bathroom.

She had snapped the towel rod in half.

"They all become selfish and ungrateful. I lose trust in them, and then I move on to another city."

I tried to probe her mind to read her thoughts, but my telepathy failed, as it often did with vampires. It was a shame because I knew she was withholding powerful secrets.

She whirled around to face me again. I jumped, startled.

"Will you take away the hope magic?" she begged, her eyes blazing with predatory power.

"I don't know how to, and I don't want to. Taking away hope goes against everything the Goddess stands for."

She gave a low growl and looked away.

"I'll return your bracelet, though," I said in a cheery voice.

"No need." She raised her left hand. The snake bangle rested around her forearm.

I instinctively felt for my pocket. It was empty, of course.

"How did you get that?"

She laughed. "You should understand by now how special I am."

I did, though I refused to let her know it.

She touched the serpent bracelet and slid it up and down her wrist.

"How I loved this silly bangle at one time," she said. "When I met Aastacki, he said the design was inspired by him, that vain, vain angel."

"Why do you call the Father of Lies by his Fae name?"

"Faeries settled the land where I was born before humans came along." She looked at me archly. "It is said the Fae are the children of Danu, if you didn't know. Aastacki told me the story of the first humans living in a garden, tempted by a serpent. The serpent was Aastacki. The humans listened to his lies and were cast out of paradise. Yet, I listened to his lies, too."

"What lies?"

"He told me he loved me. I was newly married then and told him I was taken. He promised me if I left my husband, I would live with Aastacki in paradise." She laughed bitterly. "Later, my husband died in battle, and I died of the fever—my daughter, too. On my deathbed, Aastacki promised me eternal life if I gave

120

my soul to him. I did. But what he gave me instead was eternal un-death."

She grasped one piece of the broken towel rod and fingered its splintered end, then tapped it against her ribcage as if she were fantasizing about staking herself.

"Aastacki didn't know what it was like to be a vampire. He enchanted the bracelet to give me the power to mesmerize my prey. But I soon learned how to do it myself, as most vampires do. I would have thrown this bracelet into the sea had it not been for Danu taking pity on me and filling it with the power of hope. Too late, I learned I was bound to the bracelet and imprisoned by the hope."

"No, hope sets you free," I said.

Another bitter laugh.

"Not for me. I am imprisoned by hope in this world where I have known only loss. Please, I implore you, free me from this false hope."

"It's not false. You must have wrong expectations or the wrong perspective."

"Don't tell me I'm wrong." Her nostrils flared with anger, and her red hair seemed to have a halo from the ceiling light. "You're just an ignorant human. You haven't spent thousands of years searching and finding nothing, facing emptiness and loss. I just want to forget it all. Free me from this hope."

"I don't know how." What I said was true. If Danu wanted me to break the magic, she would have come to me in a vision and told me so. "Even if I could do it, I wouldn't. I believe in hope. It's a fundamental part of my being. Hope brings new beginnings, and they are what have kept me going throughout my life—as short as it may seem to you. Heck, even this inn, The Esperanza Inn, is named after hope."

I guess Lethia decided to change tactics from begging to

threatening. She suddenly was in my face, looming over me, and forcing me to push the small of my back into the pedestal sink.

"I demand that you grant me my wish. If you do not, by next sundown, I will strike against the guilds. And against someone you care about."

The claustrophobia of her looming over me lessened as her mass seemed to lessen. Soon, I could see through her to the bathroom door. She quickly faded away and was gone.

Leaving me to wonder if I had made a big mistake by not doing what she wanted.

MOST PEOPLE WOULD HAVE RUSHED FROM THE BATHROOM TO tell their loved ones about the vampire who had appeared in there. Not me. You know me well enough not to be surprised. Nope, I remained in the bathroom and snatched the two pieces of the towel rod.

I'm a psychometrist, and I had a job to do.

Fortunately, there were not a bunch of unrelated memories cluttering up the wooden rod. No one handles towel rods, only the towels that hang on them. The only memories I detected were Lethia's.

The wood practically burned with her frustration as I grasped both pieces. She was angry at the probability that I would not cooperate. When she first handled the rod, I was asking about—

—*my followers. Yes, there were thousands of them by now. Once, they practically worshipped me. Now, they despise me. All because of the paranoia caused by Aastacki whispering in my ear that they do not love me and are plotting against me. When I can no longer trust them, I lash out, punishing them for minor offenses. Which makes them resent me.*

And the resentment creates more paranoia in me, and I crack down even harder.

Until I can no longer be their Nest Mother and must move on to another town or village and start anew.

The mother instinct in me—the instinct cut off at its strongest point—drives me to create more vampire children. As if they could substitute for my loss. Of course, they don't.

And time and again, I let Aastacki's lies poison my mind and alienate my followers. Why can't I resist him? What is so intoxicating about the fear and paranoia and hatred he stirs in my heart?

It condemns me to be being alone forever!

SNAP—

—went the towel rod, and the pieces clattered to the tile floor.

But I had learned quite a bit more than I had expected.

Now, I concentrated on the piece with the sharp, splintered end. The memory of her fondling it, holding it to her heart, as if she were thinking—

—If only I could push it through my skin and end this all without having to beg this stupid half-human, half-goddess to help me.

But I can't.

Because of the hope—that my existence will be happier, and I will be less lonely.

And, most of all, that I will find her. Hope that Aastacki lied when he said he couldn't bring her back after the fever took us both—that she is out there somewhere waiting for me.

But every day, I suspect that this hope is as false as Aastacki's lies. It's like a potion that clouds my judgement and makes me believe ridiculous things, stringing me along like a fool.

If the hope is false, once it is gone, I will see the truth. Then, I'll know what to do. Continue searching or take my own life.

I suspect it will be the latter.

Oh, I will be so enraged if Danu does not grant me my wish. I will—

—drop the wood onto the floor.

She never completed her thought. But I had a feeling about how powerful her rage would be. And I was scared.

THAT NIGHT AS I LAY IN BED, CORY SNORING BESIDE ME, MY mind called out to the Mother Goddess.

Please tell me what to do. Lethia wants me to take away the hope you gave her. Will you consent to her wish? Will you give me the power to do so?

No answer.

It just seemed so wrong to kill hope. It was against everything the Goddess and I stood for.

But if Lethia was suffering that badly, wouldn't extinguishing hope be a form of mercy?

Tell me, Mother Goddess. Please tell me what to do. Or intervene. I'm happy for you to solve this problem.

I heard nothing but silence.

And snoring.

"SHE HAD A CHILD AND I BELIEVE SHE'S TRYING TO FIND HER," I told my fellow Memory Guild members in the torch-lit virtual stone hall.

"Are you serious?" Summer asked.

"She didn't leave a direct memory, only inferences. But she told me some sort of fever or plague killed her and her young daughter. Aastacki claimed he could only bring Lethia back to life—not her daughter. But Lethia didn't believe him. The hope that Danu gave her is making her try to find her daughter."

"Why would Aastacki mislead her about her daughter?" Laurel asked.

"To maintain power over her," Dr. Noordlun suggested.

I nodded in agreement. I speculated that her strong motherly instinct partly explains why she creates so many new vampire children. Perhaps elders like her naturally need many followers. And in her case, it's also because she continually needs to rebuild her followers after she alienates them because of the Father of Lies' influence.

"If you don't mind my guessing some more," I continued, "I believe she continually takes over new territories in order to find out if her daughter is there."

"If her daughter was brought back to life as Lethia was, she'd be a vampire, of course," Diego said. "I don't believe we have any child vampires in San Marcos."

"Thank heavens," Diana muttered.

"Can the powers and resources of the Memory Guild help find the daughter?" I asked.

"Why would we want to help Lethia?" Laurel said.

"To exert leverage over her," Dr. Noordlun said.

"And make her leave us alone," I added.

CHAPTER 14

DOUBLE THE JUBBLES
TROUBLES

"Hello, I'm Mr. Hendrik Jubbles' niece. I have come looking for him."

I smiled weakly at the stout, serious, forty-something woman with the thick glasses and boyish hairstyle. I should have known this day would come.

"Mr. Jubbles checked out days ago. Such a lovely guest he was. We truly appreciate our repeat guests."

"He didn't return home. He left me in charge of caring for his bird, so I'm positive he never came back."

"Good heavens. I hope he's okay."

Of course, he wasn't okay. He was a newly created vampire who hadn't yet gotten over the trauma of his transition. I didn't know where he currently was—with Lethia somewhere. As far as I was concerned, he was out of my hair. I had finally checked him out and moved his personal articles to a storage room in case he came back for them. After all, even vampires need a change of clothes, deodorant, and toothpaste.

I had no information regarding his next-of-kin, and he had

never mentioned any friends or family. He had given me the impression that he never married and was a content elderly bachelor, staying in bed-and-breakfast inns in small towns and shopping for antiques—while drinking too heavily each night.

Now, I felt guilty for moving on and consigning Mr. Jubbles to memory. Come to think of it, he wouldn't have been turned into a vampire if he hadn't been staying with me when Lethia came calling. And if he hadn't broken into the storage closet to snatch cocktail peanuts.

"Your uncle did leave a few possessions here," I admitted under the weight of guilt.

"Why would he do that?" Her brow furrowed beneath her eyeglasses.

"He left in a great hurry. Overnight. I don't know why. We were going to ship his belongings to his home address but didn't know if he would need them elsewhere."

"This is quite peculiar. My name is Debbie, by the way. Debbie Jubbles."

"Darla Chesswick. Pleased to meet you. I wish it were under better circumstances."

"Indeed." She gave a fake smile, revealing a wide gap in her front teeth. I found it disconcerting. "First, I wish to see his room."

This flummoxed me. "Another guest is in his room now. Remember, he left several days ago."

"Then, I would like to examine his possessions."

When I first met her, Debbie seemed as if she were simply making casual inquiries. Now, she had a serious tone.

"Did you come to San Marcos solely to look for Mr. Jubbles?"

"Yes. My father—his brother—is very concerned. And it just so happens that I'm a private investigator by trade. So, I'm taking on the case pro bono."

Great. Freaking great. With all the problems I'm dealing with, now I must hide what happened to Mr. Jubbles from a P.I.?

"Of course, I'll help you in any way I can. I happen to be very busy right now, so. . ."

"No worries. I have a reservation here, so I can devote my time twenty-four-seven to finding what happened to dear Uncle Hendrik."

"You have a reservation?" I didn't recall a new Jubbles calling us.

"I made it online."

Pulling it up in my booking software, I found it. And noted she would be here an entire week. I broke out in a sweat.

"Let me check you in and let you get settled."

"No hurry with that. I'd like to see his belongings now, please."

For years now, I've remained standing astride the normal and supernatural worlds, like a woman on a frozen lake with her feet on two ice sheets. The ice sheets were now drifting apart.

I led Debbie to a storage closet near the utility room where we keep luggage for people who arrive before their room is ready or accidentally leave bags behind. Mr. Jubbles' suitcase and shoulder bag sat in the rear corner.

"Help yourself." I pointed to the bags and held my breath.

Debbie opened the main bag. "His stuff looks like it was simply thrown in here. I can't believe he would do that."

"Maybe he was in a hurry."

"Everything is in here, including his toilet kit. He must have left the inn with absolutely nothing."

"We believe it was in the middle of the night." This was the first complete truth I'd told her.

She searched his shoulder bag. "All his antiquing literature is in here. Aha—a list of the shops he planned to visit. This could be helpful."

"Do you mind if I look at that?" I was curious if Mom's store was on his list.

It was. The store's name, Elegant Eras, was crossed off the list with the notation, "Mostly junk."

Mr. Jubbles was an astute customer.

"I'm going to take this list and make inquiries at every store. Are there any guests registered who were here when Uncle Hendrik was?"

"Not at the moment."

"I will need to speak to your entire staff."

"Okay. There aren't many of us—just my husband, daughter, and me. Plus two housekeepers. I'll tell them to make time for you."

"Thank you. One last question for now: Uncle Hendrik is quite the bon vivant, and I wonder if he overindulged—"

"I'm afraid, yes. Both times he has stayed here. He never caused any problems, but I assumed his love for wine and spirits might have contributed to his unusual departure."

Debbie nodded with a grave expression.

"First, I should check with the police and the hospital."

"Good idea. I should have done so myself."

The truth was, I called Detective Samson the moment I found Mr. Jubbles exsanguinated in the supply closet. When it turned out that he was undead, not dead, Samson and I wisely kept the police out of it. But I can't mention that.

Which, I'm sure, makes me look very suspicious to Debbie Jubbles, Private Investigator.

"Oh, and one last question," she said.

"I thought you'd already asked me your last question."

"They just keep popping into my head. Do you have security cameras inside the inn?"

"No. Only outside, to prevent break-ins and muggings. Any facility that has cameras indoors isn't doing it to protect its guests. It's protecting itself from liability. If you want to see the outdoor footage from when your uncle was here, I'll send you a link to it."

I'd already gone through the footage. Through my escapades with supernatural entities, I've learned the entities rarely show up on video. That was the case here. There is footage of Mr. Jubbles returning to the inn in the late afternoon of his last day as a human, but not of him leaving as a vampire. Lethia doesn't appear, either. Debbie will have fun trying to figure how her uncle left the inn.

I had no intention of helping her learn the truth.

AT THE NEXT MEETING OF THE MEMORY GUILD, I LISTENED to what our archivists had learned so far about Lethia.

"I've been contacting other vampire guilds and associations in Florida and elsewhere," Diego said. "It appears that prior to coming to San Marcos, Lethia was in Savannah, Georgia."

"She likes old cities," Archibald said. "Though America is sorely lacking in those compared to Europe."

"Only when you speak of human settlements," Summer said. "Elves have had towns here almost as long as the Native Americans—far longer than many European towns."

"And there have been Fae here even longer," Baldric said.

"Of course, of course," Archibald sputtered. I was speaking of *human* cities because vampires come from humans. No reason for a gargoyle like me to be touting human achievements."

I wanted to remind him that humans had carved him before he became enchanted, but wisely thought better of it.

"Back to my report," Diego said. "What I heard confirms what Darla learned from Lethia's memories: Lethia is her own worst enemy."

"Please be specific," Dr. Noordlun said.

"To echo what Archibald said, vampires keep many of the flaws we had as humans. We can be selfish, childish, and irrational. From the outside, it appeared the Clan of the Eternal Night was all of one mind, unified because of our vampirism." His face clouded over. "We were, at least, before the spell that affected most of us. The truth is, it is difficult for a vampire leader to inspire mutual trust and compassion among vampires. My contact in Savannah told me Lethia failed miserably at it with the family of followers she was building.

"Rather than bringing all her followers together, she used division to exert power over them," Diego continued. "She pitted one against the other, spreading false rumors and disparaging them all behind their backs. While they fought each other, she found it easier to rule them. But only for a time."

"Her approach was influenced by the Father of Lies," I said. "Aastacki, as she calls him."

"That is what the Father of Lies has been doing with humans since the beginning."

We all murmured our agreement.

Diego went on. "Her followers grew, but so did conflict between them. The Hostess City Vampire's Guild grew concerned about the unruliness of these new vampires joining their ranks. Rumors began to spread about plots to depose Lethia. Which only made her more paranoid, lashing out against those she believed were disloyal. Instead of frightening them all into submission, it created more rebellion. Finally, a disturbing element forced the guild to step in."

Everyone looked at Diego expectantly, though I had a suspicion of what he was going to say.

"Lethia began turning young children—girls, specifically."

Diana and Lauren gasped.

"Yes," Diego said, "all vampire guilds and associations have strict rules against turning children under sixteen. Many have raised the age to eighteen. Turning young children, like what Lethia was doing, is especially forbidden. You can't even attack them for a quick bite when you're starving."

"She's acting out of longing for her missing child," I said.

"That is only speculation," Dr. Noordlun said.

"I know, but I read her memories and feel certain it is true."

"A group of her followers attacked her," Diego said, "but she's too powerful. She destroyed them easily. The guild quickly banished her from the city. A few followers accompanied her, but eventually abandoned her and made their ways back to Savannah."

"What a twisted monster she is," James said.

"And sad, too," I murmured.

"I want to know why she has such a close relationship with the Father of Lies," said Dr. Noordlun. "He is our greatest enemy. Another reason to get rid of her."

"How do we learn more about whether she had a child who died?" I asked him.

"If Lethia existed during the time of Danu, that was thousands of years ago. There are very few specific mentions of Danu in historical texts. Her era left nothing behind as historical records. In conventional ways, that is."

"Do the Tugara have memories of those times?"

"Yes." He smiled. "The earliest history of humankind was

oral, aside from an occasional cave painting or stone carving. History—memories—were passed down verbally from generation to generation, often becoming distorted or forgotten. But as you know, Darla, memories don't always disappear when the mind that held them does. The memories were out there, and the Tugara absorbed them. Thanks to the earliest members of the Memory Guild, we have the Tugara in our care. I've been trying to find information about Lethia in the Tugara's memories, but it is extremely daunting. I won't stop trying, though, until I learn something useful."

"How do you define useful?" Archibald asked.

"If it helps us get rid of this vampire. And perhaps even land a blow on the Father of Lies."

"Good luck with that one, old chap."

AFTER I ASTRAL TRAVELLED BACK TO THE INN, I HAD JUST enough time to prep for the evening Wine Hour. Cory was busy fixing—or trying to fix—a plumbing leak in 302. Sophie was nowhere to be found. This was becoming common with her, ever since Haarg came into her life.

Never mind, hosting the Wine Hour was easy for one person to do: you slice cheese and fruit, lay out crackers, heat the canapés, and uncork bottles of wine. I could do it with my eyes closed. Especially the uncorking part.

This Wine Hour was going to be much more difficult, however. Because my first guest to arrive was Debbie Jubbles.

"I haven't yet canvassed the antique shops, because all the suspicious clues are here at your inn." She took a deep sip of Cabernet and pretentiously swirled it in her mouth as if she really cared about its subtle notes.

"According to your security video, Uncle Hendrik last entered the inn at four fifty-nine p.m. On the twelfth."

"He was very punctual when it came to Wine Hour."

"There is no record of him ever leaving the inn again."

"Sometimes, there are gaps in the footage. Some sort of computer-memory-resetting technical stuff."

She ignored me. "You checked him out five days later, even though all his belongings were still in his room."

I couldn't think of a better excuse than the fact his booking had run its course. I told her that.

"He has gone missing, but you never reported it to the police."

"I didn't think he was *missing*. Besides, I'm not a family member. I can't go to the police unless I suspect a crime."

"He never left the inn again, and you pretended he had checked out. I, for one, suspect a crime. And it looks as if it was committed in your inn."

If draining a person of blood to the point of death before bringing him back as a vampire was a crime—and I'm pretty sure it should be—then Debbie was right. But I couldn't tell her that.

"I'm afraid I must go to the police about this," she said, giving me the stink eye.

"Wouldn't you like to try a canapé first?"

CHAPTER 15

VOCIFEROUS VAMP

"If anyone is going to make vampires go public, it's her." I had Samson on the phone, venting about Debbie Jubbles. "She's like a pit bull with a chew toy. Nothing will make her let go of this."

"Maybe you should let her meet her uncle and let him decide if he should tell her the truth about himself or not."

"First, I don't know where he is. Second, he hasn't finished his transition. I don't trust him to behave rationally. His niece said she's filed a missing person report. What do we do if she tries to get me charged with his murder?"

"Don't get ahead of yourself. Let's take this one step at a time. Hopefully, she'll get frustrated and give up."

He didn't know Debbie. Nor did I. She was even more tenacious than I imagined.

As I walked past the parlor that afternoon, voices came from within. Inside, Debbie and Officer Fernandez sat across from each other in the wingback reading chairs. The cop wrote furiously in her notebook while Debbie recited the litany of suspicious facts about Mr. Jubbles' disappearance.

"The guests at this inn drop like flies, I tell you," Fernandez said.

"That is not true," I interrupted. "Don't tarnish my inn's reputation."

"Let's just say I'm never surprised when I get a report about this place."

"You've had other guests go missing?" Debbie asked me.

"Well, just one. It turns out he was a hit man who intended to kill me." I left out the part about him getting eaten by dragons in the In Between.

Fernandez rolled her eyes. "You didn't mention your deceased guests."

"There really weren't that many. Hotels have fatalities all the time."

"You have, what, eleven rooms? Your rate of fatalities makes this place more like a hospice than a hotel."

"Will you knock it off with the sarcasm?"

Fernandez stood and stuck her pad in her pocket.

"As soon as a detective is assigned to this case, you'll be contacted," she said to Debbie. "I imagine we'll have a forensics team search the facility for any signs of foul play."

I cringed. I hadn't seen any blood on the floor of the supply closet where Mr. Jubbles was attacked, but if there was even a tiny speck, the police would find it.

And I would be in a fine mess.

After Fernandez left, I asked Debbie to please be patient.

"Why?" she asked. "To give you more time to hire a good defense team?"

"Because your uncle will turn up, eventually."

"If only that were true."

Samson's suggestion about introducing Debbie to the vampire version of her uncle was looking much better to me now. In fact, it might be the only way to get me out of a murder charge.

THAT NIGHT, I NOTICED A TINY SEEDLING HAD SPROUTED IN the tile grout near the window in the cottage's bathroom. This happened all the time since the Goddess became part of me. Brushing my teeth before going to bed, I laid out in my mind all my worries and to-dos. I find this makes it less likely that worries will wake me up at three in the morning.

Okay, besides having Debbie Jubbles more or less accuse me of murdering her uncle, I had Lethia demanding that I undo the Goddess's hope magic. Or else. I didn't believe it was the right thing to do, but I needed Danu's guidance, or at least that of Birog, the Druid spirit who occasionally gave me advice.

On top of all that, there were the infected vampires to cure, and the mayhem caused by Lethia to be stopped. My daughter wanted to marry a Fae war god, and I didn't know how we could afford to pay for a wedding fit for a god. Plus, was this match even a good idea?

Finally, there was the tear in the Veil that needed fixing. Every time a monster came through, it put the people of San Marcos at risk. I didn't think this should be my responsibility, but no one else was taking it on.

Whew! Was that everything? No, there were overdue bills to pay and complications with our taxes. Plus, I felt like I was coming down with something, and my phone has been acting up.

Years ago, these last few worries would wake me up. Now, they were nothing compared to the other matters hanging over my head.

So, would I be able to sleep now that I had enumerated all my concerns?

Doubtful.

Before I clicked off the bathroom light, I felt a tingle of magic in the air. I hoped Birog or, even, the Goddess was about to make an appearance.

Instead of a messenger bringing needed advice, an entity materialized between me and the bathroom door.

It was Lethia.

"Why do you always visit me in the bathroom?" I asked.

"Have you considered my request?"

"I'm waiting for word from Danu."

"Waiting? But she is part of you?"

"It's not like I have a direct line to her. She only enlightens me when she wants to."

"I have no patience for her whims."

"With all due respect, you've been around for thousands of years. What's the rush?"

That wasn't the wisest question to ask, I realized as I dangled two feet above the floor with her hand around my throat.

"You slow-witted human, I will repeat to you one more time only. Take this curse of hope away from me. Clear my eyes of the gauzy sentimentality of wishful thinking. Allow me to see the truth. If I still want to end my existence and erase my memories, I will be able to do so."

She lowered me to the floor and released her vise grip on my windpipe. I coughed as I wheezed air into my lungs.

"You've made yourself very clear," I said.

"If you don't give me what I want, I will continue to lead the infected vampires in wiping out your stupid guilds, as Aastacki wishes, and I will rule over the city and the countryside. And you will suffer. I will harm the humans you care about most."

"Okay. Got it. But one thing before you go."

Her thin red eyebrows arched in surprise that I would make a request.

"Can you please tell Mr. Jubbles that his niece is here and would like to see him?"

She snorted with disdain as she faded away.

The tiny seedling by the window had shriveled and died.

JUST BECAUSE OUR ATTEMPTS TO BREAK THE SPELL THAT infected the vampires hadn't worked didn't mean we were going to stop trying. In fact, Sophie and I invited ourselves to a special working session of the top magicians of the Magic Guild held at the automotive shop owned by Baldric.

He was one of the few individuals, like Diego, who belonged to more than one guild. He was the leader of the Guild of Fae and Wee People, but, as a powerhouse in Fae magic, he also was a member of the Magic Guild. Arch Mage Bob was there, of course, as were a half dozen of the top mages, wizards, and witches.

Baldric's auto shop specialized in Italian sports cars. It wasn't the kind of business you'd expect a faerie to own, but go figure. With its expansive concrete floor and bays cleared of cars, it was a good place to work on often-messy magic spells. Well, it was if you didn't think about the flammable liquids stored here.

The assembled magicians sat in a large circle of folding

chairs. I sat atop a workbench off to the side. While they brain-stormed, Bob took notes on a whiteboard perched on an easel. The symbols and formulas were as undecipherable to me as quantum physics.

"We need to stop thinking like modern hominids, dudes," Bob said. "This spell is ancient and indiscriminate. Aastacki—or a magician working for him—probably made it thousands of years ago, and it targeted any kind of creature. Not just vampires. As we know, the metal of the box that contained it has extraterrestrial origins. And the creature who fabricated it was of a species that no longer exists."

"Agreed," Baldric said. "But what does that mean for us?"

"It means, like, we got to think of really basic elemental magic. And alchemy. Nothing based on our religious belief systems and cultures. Just really, you know, basic. That last spell we tried was too complicated, in my humble opinion."

Baldric, the primary author of that spell, couldn't hide his annoyance.

"It should have worked. The execution was flawed."

"Well, it didn't work," said an elderly wizard I didn't know. "Aastacki or the Father of Lies, demon or evil god—whatever you want to call him—is more powerful than any of us. We must be creative. Both of you could be correct in your approach. Or neither of you. My intuition tells me that what brings down our foe might not be magic at all."

This set the room off into chattering and arguing.

Suddenly, Bob raised his hand.

"Something just triggered the warding spells around this building."

I tensed, and everyone in the circle stood. We all knew that Lethia had vowed to destroy the guilds, and here were several top members, all in one location. But they knew the risk and had set so many warding spells that a rat could have set them off.

But I doubted this was a rat. I searched the workbench for a stake-like tool, expecting vampires to come crashing through the windows.

None did, yet.

It painfully dawned on me that harming the guilds might not be her objective tonight. She'd also threatened to come after someone close to me.

And Sophie was here. No matter how good a fighter she'd become, she'll always be my vulnerable, sweet little daughter.

"The spell is telling me the men's room window was left open," Bob said as he walked to the far end of the building.

Something was off in the way Bob walked. He had a jerking motion, unlike the relaxed rolling gait I'd seen so often on the beach as he walked with his surfboard under his arm. His voice sounded a little strange, too.

"I thought I made sure the window was closed," Baldric said, more to himself.

The other magicians were busy covering their butts: weaving protection spells or, in the case of Sophie, preparing for battle. I didn't remember seeing her carry her sword inside, but she was busy putting a layer of magic on it.

No one noticed Bob was acting weird except for me.

It was as if he were mesmerized.

I slid off the workbench. Bob was too experienced a mage to allow himself to be mesmerized. But he'd never encountered a vampire as powerful as Lethia.

"Bob, wait!" I called as I hurried after him.

He had left the shop floor and was in the customer service and waiting area, heading for the bathrooms.

"Bob!"

He turned toward me, which was a good sign.

But when I saw his expression, my heart sank.

"Bob, you've been mesmerized. Resist the urge to go to the window. Stay right here."

He didn't listen, just continued walking through the tiny waiting room.

I grabbed his shoulder. "Bob!"

He brushed away my hand and opened the bathroom door.

Between the urinal and the stall, was a window that had been slid open. The opening looked too small for someone of Bob's size, but he grabbed the top of the frame and pulled himself up, so that he was sitting on the sill with his legs hanging outside.

"Bob! Stop!"

I ran to him, grabbed his shirt, and watched him slide through the window, landing on his feet outside. His shirt was torn where I had held it.

I looked out. Lethia waiting for him in the parking lot a few yards away. Further back in the darkness were the red glowing eyes of several of her followers.

All the layers and layers of warding spells the magicians had laid turned out to be useless. Lethia was simply too powerful.

"You are the head of the Magic Guild?" Lethia asked him.

He nodded, woodenly, as if drunk.

"Pleased to meet you. I will be your maker."

What happened next was just a blur because of its rapidity. Lethia got Bob down to his knees and sank her fangs into his neck.

I screamed. She looked up at me and smiled at me through bloody lips.

The next thing I knew, she was sprinting away from the

building with Bob over her shoulder, though he weighed more than her.

I knew Lethia would not stop at simply feeding upon him. She would turn him and make him her servant.

It bothered me the way his limp body bounced against her back as she ran. He was a friend, and he was now lost to me forever.

"I NEVER THOUGHT I WOULD INVESTIGATE A MURDER," DEBBIE said. Her voice drifted out of the breakfast room while I made sure to be within earshot.

"Let's not make assumptions," Samson's voice said. "What we have at the moment is a possible missing person situation."

"Possible? He's definitely missing."

"Ms. Jubbles, your uncle is a grown adult. He might have deliberately taken off without telling anyone. How old did you say he is?"

"Seventy-four."

"Has he shown any symptoms of dementia?"

"No. He's still sharp as a tack. When he's sober."

Bella, our main housekeeper, walked past me in the hall with a squeegee. She looked at me curiously. I waved her away. It was an almost daily occurrence to find her boss behaving oddly.

"Is it true that other guests have been murdered in this inn?" Debbie asked in the breakfast room.

"It wouldn't be my place to comment," Samson replied. "When an inn is nearly three hundred years old, people will have expired there."

"Do you investigate a lot of murders in San Marcos?"

"No. San Marcos is a very safe, small city. Shouldn't I be the one asking the questions?"

Samson wasn't quite correct. This was a safe city if you ignored all the supernatural goings on. Which the police regularly did.

"I always believed being a private investigator would be glamorous," Debbie said. "Like in the movies. Instead, all I do is uncover insurance scams and spy on cheating spouses. Uncle Hendrik is the first dark crime I've investigated."

"We don't know it was a crime. You said you were visiting the antique shops on his list?"

"I've gotten halfway through the list. Most of the shopkeepers remember him as a pain in the butt who tried to haggle at every price and then walked out without buying anything. One of them said something strange, though."

"Please go on."

"Well, she said she had to return to her shop late at night, long after it had closed. And she thought she saw Uncle Hendrik chasing a cat behind the dumpster."

"You should have mentioned this earlier. She saw him after he had disappeared?"

"That would be two days afterward. But I believe her account is mistaken."

"Why?"

"Uncle Hendrik doesn't like cats. He's allergic to them."

If he was hungry enough, it wouldn't matter, I thought.

"Well, if you want to assist this investigation—"

"I do, I do!"

"Then, please continue canvassing the antique shops. That will be invaluable to me. I'll run a search through the Florida Department of Law Enforcement and FBI databases and see if anything turns up on your uncle. You'll hear from me soon."

"Thank you, detective."

Samson walked out of the breakfast room, giving me a wry smile. Later in the day, during Teatime, Debbie glowered at me while she devoured my freshly baked scones. She truly believed I had done something to Mr. Jubbles.

The sad fact was, indirectly, I *had* done something to him. I had caused Lethia to come to the inn.

CHAPTER 16
STAIN ON MY REPUTATION

With Samson handling the "disappearance" of Mr. Jubbles —and, presumably, running interference for me—I didn't expect to find a crime-scene tech standing in the foyer.

"Can I help you?" I asked, though I recognized the skinny young man from a previous case. This was probably his first job out of the academy. And here he was, trying to bring me down.

"I'm here to do some forensics work." He looked around nervously. "Detective Samson was supposed to be here."

"Did he order the testing?"

"Um, I don't know."

I didn't want this guy prying around in my inn. It wouldn't look good to kick him out of here, though. Fortunately for him, Samson finally arrived.

"Sorry I'm late." He was covered in sweat, which wasn't a bad look for him. "A perp chose to test my sprinting stamina."

"Did you catch him?" I asked.

He glanced down at his jeans, which were covered with mud and grass stains.

"Yes. Flawless open-field tackle."

"Why is *he* here?" I nodded toward the nervous crime-scene tech.

"I got pressure from above to test for foul play. Wouldn't be surprised if it was Fernandez whispering into the captain's ear. She's always been suspicious of you."

"Yes. But it's nice to know officially that I have an enemy on the police force."

"She's not an enemy."

"She thinks I killed my guest."

"Not necessarily you. It could have been a staff member or another guest."

"You're not making me feel any better."

"What tests are you going to do?" Samson asked the tech.

"Oh, UV light and Luminol, looking for bodily fluids. If I find a location of interest, I'll look for prints, too."

And next began the most uncomfortable two hours of my life, not counting my recent colonoscopy—even though this felt more invasive.

The latest occupant of Mr. Jubbles' former room had checked out this morning, so the tech had free rein to poke around in there. He found disgusting things I won't mention— no matter how clean a hotel room is, humans leave behind "souvenirs." But more importantly, he didn't find any blood or indicators of violence.

Next, he went around in the common areas, shining his ultraviolet light everywhere. This was exceedingly awkward because guests occasionally passed by and wondered what he was doing.

"Do you have a cat?" the tech asked.

"Yes, Cervantes." I didn't mention he was also Sophie's witch's familiar.

"Looks like he's been doing some marking near the doorways."

"I'll have a word about that with him," I said. And, literally, I would.

The tech went through every room downstairs, with me following doggedly along. Samson followed, too, but at a distance, feigning disinterest.

Everything should be fine, as long as the tech didn't check the food pantry closet.

"What's in here?" he asked outside of the utility room door.

"Laundry, workshop, storage. Guests can't get in here. You need a key."

That satisfied him. He made his way back to the common areas. The breakfast room and living room had nothing macabre; neither did the courtyard.

"Do guests go into the kitchen?"

"They're not supposed to, but sometimes they do."

He snooped around in there until his back stiffened.

"Traces of blood on the island counter," he said triumphantly.

"I cut my finger there last week while mincing onions. I thought I'd cleaned it up well."

"There's barely a trace." He studied the spot with a magnifying loupe. "Yeah, not consistent with a violent injury."

When he finished the kitchen, his eyes caught the food storage closet.

"Do guests go in there?"

"Nope. It's kept locked." My heart fluttered.

"It's not fully closed." He turned the handle and opened the door. "See? There's a chance guests could get in here."

I glanced back at Samson. His face was stern, and he nodded.

His thoughts drifted into my head.

We can't impede an official investigation.

The tech turned on the light and went inside. He was very thorough, even moving boxes around.

"I found a bloodstain on the floor," he announced. "The wood did a good job of preserving it. And cocktail peanuts with blood on them."

Dang it! I thought I had done a thorough cleaning.

Now, things got serious. The tech went out to his car and returned with a bag of additional equipment.

"How do I get out of this?" I whispered to Samson.

"Once the blood is matched to Mr. Jubbles, you'll get out of this only by producing an alive Mr. Jubbles. I mean, an undead one. And he needs a convincing innocent explanation of why he spilled blood in here."

"But I don't know where he is. There's no reason to expect Lethia gave him my message to come here. And even if he does, will he say the right thing?"

"If he has fully transitioned, he'll be onboard with the rules of secrecy. But in the meantime, you need to prepare for the worst."

"What do you mean?"

"You'd better look for a defense attorney."

"You won't charge me with a crime. Will you?"

"If there's probable cause, we can arrest you. And with this forensic evidence, the DA can charge you."

"Even if there's not a body?"

"Yup. There are plenty of ways to dispose of a body. Let's hope Mr. Jubbles shows up soon."

SOMEONE WAS KNOCKING ON THE COTTAGE'S FRONT DOOR. I leaped out of bed.

"I've got this," I told Cory before throwing on a robe, hurrying through the tiny living room, and opening the door.

It was Roderick. Unlike most vampires who can adapt to new times and technologies, Roderick was still stuck in the nineteenth century. Texting or calling me on the phone was out of the question for him.

"Mr. Jubbles is paying us a visit," he announced with no show of emotion.

I followed Roderick into the inn's kitchen. A single lamp on the counter burned above a chess set. Archibald was perched on the subway tile above it.

Mr. Jubbles sat at the kitchen table in the corner, cloaked in shadows.

"I came to get my stuff," he said to me without so much as a hello.

"I'm so happy to see you! How are you doing?"

"It's been . . . difficult. I'm feeling somewhat better now than I was before. I wish I could have stayed here and hung out with Roddy and Archie."

"Don't call me Roddy. I prefer my proper name of Roderick."

"Don't call me anything other than Archibald," his chess partner warned.

"I'd even prefer living in that nasty crawlspace over where I am now."

"It is *not* nasty," Roderick said. "I clean it at least once every decade."

"Where are you staying?" I asked.

"Oh, I've been commanded not to say. I'm part of a nest that keeps growing and I'm not used to the lack of privacy. To be honest—and please don't repeat this—I am not fond of my maker. She's a very suspicious and manipulative mistress."

"So I've heard. Your niece, Debbie, is staying here. She came to find you after you didn't return home. She'll be thrilled to see you."

"Oh, I don't want to see her."

"But you must. The thing is, she suspects I murdered you. We need to show her you're alive."

Three supernatural faces stared at me like I'd committed the world's worst faux pas.

"Sorry. We need to show her you exist. In an animated form. Um, you know."

"I'm not the uncle she knew."

"Yes, you are. Just because your body temperature is several degrees lower doesn't mean you're not her beloved Uncle Hendrik."

He shook his head. "She'll spot something is off about me."

"We vampires have nothing 'off' about us," Roderick said.

"We're walking, talking corpses."

"Oh, please! You clearly haven't adjusted to your transition. As a vampire, you are faster and stronger than your pathetic human version. Your senses are more acute. Your mind is sharper."

"I don't know about the mind part," Archibald said.

Roderick ignored him. "Plus, you are immortal! Every human wants to be immortal. You are vastly superior to humans in every way."

"I can't sunbathe anymore."

"Who cares? The sun gives you cancer. The moon doesn't."

"I'm deathly pale."

"And much more handsome now. The truth is female humans find vampires irresistibly sexy."

Now, three faces stared at him with incredulity.

"Well, they do in novels and movies."

"I really, really need you to say hello to your niece, Mr.

Jubbles. Just tell her you went on a bender for a while, and spilled some blood in the pantry, but you're fine now. All you need to do is pretend that you're a living human. Vampires can do that easily."

"I don't know."

Roderick cleared his throat. "Listen to me, Mr. Jubbles. The first rule of being a vampire is: don't let humans know you're a vampire. We must keep our existence completely secret. Or humans will become alarmed and go around staking all of us. You're whining about being undead, but you really don't want to be permanently dead. Which is what you'll be after they drive a stake into your heart. And yes, it will hurt. Badly."

Mr. Jubbles shuddered.

"And if you don't let your niece know you're walking around and not buried in a landfill," I said, "I will be charged with your murder. That is not right."

"I never said you killed me. Lethia did."

"But she's a vampire and officially doesn't exist! The police can never know you were attacked and turned by a vampire. In the police's eyes, the only explanation for your disappearance, and blood on the floor of the storage closet, is murder."

"I see."

"And why were you stealing snacks in the storage closet, anyway?"

"I get the munchies at night. Well, I did when I was human. Now, my cravings are different. . ."

"Will you meet with your niece, Mr. Jubbles?"

"Okay," he said, resigned. "I will."

"I'll bring her downstairs. Roderick and Archibald, please make yourselves scarce."

I rushed upstairs and pounded on Debbie's door.

"It's Darla. Your uncle returned!"

The door opened. Debbie wore a flannel nightgown, a sleeping mask pushed up on her forehead, and a skeptical frown.

"He what?"

"He's downstairs. Apparently, he went on a bender and was too embarrassed to talk about it. He came back to collect his things and was delighted to find out you're here."

"Are you playing tricks on me?"

"Of course not. Come downstairs, and say hi to him. But remember, he's very embarrassed."

She promised she'd be downstairs shortly. Mr. Jubbles and I waited in awkward silence. Debbie finally appeared, still wearing her skeptical frown.

When she saw him sitting at the kitchen table, her expression turned to astonishment.

"Uncle Hendrik?"

"Debbie. You're looking good."

I wished he would at least pretend to be happy to see her. Instead, he looked at her with an unemotional assessment.

She went over and hugged him briefly. You could tell they weren't a hugging family.

"Oh, you're chilled to the bone, Uncle. Are you feeling okay?"

"Just a little hungover. You look good."

"You already said that. You look . . . different."

"Sobriety, my dear. I've gone cold turkey. I'm struggling a bit with the withdrawal."

Good answer. And she seemed to buy it.

"Uncle, did you cut yourself and bleed in the pantry next door?"

"I did. I was going for a late-night snack and cut my finger on a can of peanuts."

"The peanuts come in plastic containers," she said. "I saw them in the pantry."

"The sharpest containers you'll ever come across. Downright dangerous. I'm surprised the company hasn't been sued out of existence."

"I accept no legal liability," I said. Yeah, I know, that was lame. Stop frowning at me, everyone.

"It's so good to see you're all right, Mr. Jubbles," I said. "I'll get your luggage, and you can move on to greater things."

"I guess I already did."

I put my finger against my lips, hoping Debbie didn't see me.

"Are you sure you're okay, Uncle Hendrik?"

"I'm fine. And you sure look good."

"Why do you keep saying that?"

"I mean, although you're middle-aged, you have so much vitality."

"What do you mean, 'middle-aged'?"

"Nothing. Your age doesn't matter. You're deliciously healthy."

"He's having symptoms of withdrawal," I whispered to Debbie.

She might have believed me if Mr. Jubbles hadn't bared his fangs at her. I guess he couldn't resist the predatory urge.

Debbie wasn't the type to scream. But she didn't hide her shock.

"Why do you have fangs?"

"They're not fangs," I said. "You know, when you get older, your gums recede, and—"

"They're freaking fangs! Like vampire fangs! What is wrong with you, Uncle?"

"Sorry," he said, covering his mouth with his hand as if he were caught in the middle of eating a salad.

The problem was, he followed that with a low, feral growl. Debbie did finally scream.

"Nothing going on here," I said, mostly to myself.

Mr. Jubbles growled again, and Debbie backed away toward the door.

"Look, the main thing is your uncle is not dead," I said to Debbie. "So, you can cancel your report with the police."

She shook her head, tears streaming down her cheeks.

"He's a vampire. You made him a vampire."

"I didn't make him a vampire. I mean, he's *not* a vampire. Vampires don't exist."

"I need to report this to someone," she said, completely becoming unglued. "How do you report a vampire?"

"The police won't believe you," I said, trying to be helpful. "I suggest you don't worry about your uncle's receding gums, and go home, mission accomplished. Your uncle is alive and well. Congratulations!"

Meanwhile, Mr. Jubbles was staring at her neck and drooling. He needs a lot more training before he's ready for prime time. Too bad Lethia wouldn't take the time to do it.

Debbie was hyperventilating. "I'm-I'm-I'm going to call nine-one-one."

She pulled her phone from her back pocket and dropped it.

The sudden motion made Mr. Jubbles lunge at the phone like a cat to a toy. This was turning out worse than when Debbie believed I was a murderer.

Debbie screamed and ran from the room. Stairs thudded as she went upstairs back to her room, too panicked to wait for the elevator.

"Great, Mr. Jubbles. I guess you haven't learned the concept of restraint."

"I'm hungry," he whined, as if I would sympathize with him.

"I don't care. Secrecy is critical for supernaturals. And you blew it, big time. You didn't even mesmerize her into forgetting this."

"I don't know how."

I sighed. It wasn't fair to blame him for being a neglected vampire child. But this was going to have serious repercussions. Debbie wasn't the type to walk away from what she just saw.

Mr. Jubbles was eyeing my neck lustfully.

"Don't even think about it," I scolded. "I'm wearing vampire-repellant charms, and you'll just hurt yourself if you're stupid enough to attack me. I suggest you take your stuff and never come back here. Believe it or not, I might be the only one who will fight to keep you from getting staked when word gets out about you vampires."

"You sure look good," he said.

I shook my head. He was hopeless.

CHAPTER 17

FIGHT OF THE CENTURY

Sophie sobbed with an intensity I hadn't witnessed since she was young.

I sat on the edge of her bed holding my daughter, her wet face pressed into the crook of my neck.

"How could we let her take Arch Mage Bob?" she asked.

It was all I could do to keep from bawling myself. A hot, fat tear inched along my cheekbone.

"I hate that vicious old vampire!" Sophie said, her lips moving on my shoulder. "I want to sever her head and stake her."

Frankly, so did I, though I had a degree of sympathy for Lethia. Seeing the anguish in her eyes when she begged me to release her from hope left an impact on me. I guess I felt sorry for her for her loneliness and alienation. For losing her daughter.

"She's under the influence of the Father of Lies," I said. "He's the one who originally made her a vampire. And he commanded her to attack the guilds."

"I want Haarg to kill him."

"Well, I don't know if gods can be killed."

"Then, I want Haarg to hurt him as much as possible, weaken him, humiliate him."

"Breaking his spell that infected the vampires is the most important thing. If the vampires of San Marcos returned to their senses, they could band together again and drive Lethia away."

"Or kill her."

I didn't mention that her wish was Lethia's, too.

Sophie lifted her face from my shoulder.

"Haarg," she whispered. "Please, I need you."

Simply calling his name was not enough to summon a god to our modern, material world. Sophie knew this and got up from her bed, sat on the floor in a lotus position, and cast a spell that was a combination of human elemental witchcraft and the magic she'd learned from the Fae.

A tingle went down my arms from the magic in the air.

"Oh, Haarg, you offered to fight to protect me," she said in a soft voice that gradually grew louder. "I call upon you to fulfill your promise. Aastacki, the Father of Lies, has directed his vampire to harm all of us in the guilds. She has taken my mentor and friend. And soon, she will come for me. You must punish Aastacki and make him reverse the damage he has done. I beg this of you. If you love me like you say you do, you will fight him to defend my honor. And save my life."

She was silent for a while. Then she smiled and nodded. Waving her hands to break the spell, she looked up at me.

"He has challenged Aastacki to combat. And invited us to witness it for human history."

I realized I was invited to accompany Sophie because I was a member of the Memory Guild. It seems the gods rely on humans to chronicle and archive the exploits of gods. After all, they wouldn't be gods if there were no bards to sing about them.

Where would this battle take place? It's not like it was when the earth was young, and gods strode upon the same ground as humans before retreating to their Olympus or Valhalla or whichever divine retreat they called their own. Today, the gods must visit the material world in more subtle ways—disguised as an animal, appearing in visions, or showing up for dinner as a young man who's in love with your daughter.

Nowadays, gods cannot battle one another in our modern world. For an epic god vs. god battle, you had to go to neutral ground, where few humans could witness the fight.

You had to wage war in the In Between.

AN ANGEL APPEARED IN SOPHIE'S BEDROOM. NO, IT WASN'T A cute dude with white wings. It manifested itself as a shimmering in the air that obscured my view of the furniture behind it, as if I were looking through a waterfall.

It was an example of the phenomena we call gateways. They serve as portals to the In Between, but also transport living creatures to other locations on earth, both in the present and back in time to earlier eras in history. I once believed gateways were miracles of physics. It was a long time before I realized they were angels.

And yes, angels can present themselves to us as the gorgeous creatures from Renaissance paintings. But that's only to match what we want to believe they look like.

Did angels actually look like the shimmering gateways, or was their natural form something different? I might never know.

A familiar nausea filled my stomach, caused by my proximity to the gateway. I figured it had something to do with the molecular mayhem my body was about to undergo to be transported to another plane of existence.

You wouldn't think angels would make you nauseous, but there you go.

"What name may I call you?" I asked the gateway, as if speaking to a cabbie or ride-share driver.

"Raphael," a voice said in my head.

"Good to see you again." Raphael was the angel who had explained the tear in the Veil to me.

I took a deep breath and stepped into the gateway, Sophie right behind me—

And dropped a few feet, landing hard upon sandy, rocky ground. Sophie landed beside me, losing her balance, and ending up on all fours.

Not exactly the white-glove treatment you'd expect from angels, but life isn't always what you'd expect.

I looked around. We were in an area that reminded me of the Grand Canyon. We had landed atop a mesa, about the size of a football field, that towered above deep canyons extending far below. The rocks and sands were reddish brown, giving me the feeling of being on Mars.

Mars. The Roman god of war. How appropriate.

Tension filled the air. It was not just from the anticipation inside Sophie and me. It was all around us from the deities who were arriving here in the In Between.

We couldn't see them but sensed their mighty powers. It seemed as if the entire pantheon of Fae gods and even ancient gods of various human cultures were there. There were angels and demons, too. They all came to watch the fight, as if it were a high-stakes boxing match in Vegas.

"Is Haarg here?" I asked. "I don't see him."

"He will show himself for sure," Sophie replied. "For him, the honor and glory of victory is as important as winning itself."

Then a human head rose from the canyon below us—the

massive head of a giant. Haarg stood on the canyon floor in human form, yet his size was colossal, nearly as tall as the mesa we were standing on. He was clad in only a loincloth and looked even more muscular than when he came over for dinner. He reminded me more of a comic-book superhero than a god. I could see why Sophie found him sexy, to put it mildly.

On his belt was a short sword, and in his hands was a sling.

A thunderclap shook the ground. When I saw the giant dragon approaching, I realized the thunder came from its beating wings.

"The dragon is Aastacki, the Father of Lies," Sophie said. "Trying to play games with Haarg's head."

As the dragon approached him, Haarg crouched and swung his sling in a circular motion several times before releasing a boulder at the dragon. When it hit the flying lizard, the creature disappeared.

"Come back and fight with honor!" Haarg shouted, his voice echoing throughout the canyon.

I knew the Father of Lies didn't possess an ounce of honor.

Haarg's right jaw shifted sideways, and his head snapped to the side. He staggered, trying to regain his balance.

"Cheater!" Sophie shouted. "Aastacki is attacking him while invisible!"

Haarg dodged, and his shoulder bent as an invisible blow hit it. He seemed to get a sense of his opponent's movements now, though.

Haarg suddenly lunged with his sword, and blood sprayed against the canyon wall.

Sophie cheered; I felt mildly ill. I regretted coming here.

Haarg furiously parried an invisible weapon. A gash appeared on his naked chest, but he ignored it and went on the offense.

A quick chopping motion of his sword caused another spray

of blood. Now, Haarg pressed ever forward. Based on Haarg's position, his invisible enemy must be trapped in a corner of the canyon wall.

Haarg lunged, and his sword struck the rock wall. He stepped back and looked around fruitlessly. Aastacki had somehow escaped.

"Cheater!" shouted Sophie.

Not to defend Aastacki, but the Father of Lies should not be expected to fight in a straightforward manner.

In fact, I was confused when I saw there were now two Haargs in the canyon—both identical, including the gashes on their chests.

They collided like Sumo wrestlers, then fell upon each other with savage thrusts and chops of their swords, steel ringing against steel.

A buzz rose from the unseen audience of ancient gods.

As the two Haargs struggled in the canyon, one gaining the upper hand and then the other, I lost track of which was the original one. I could only imagine how disturbing it must have been for Haarg trying to kill his own mirror image.

And then, in a blink, the second Haarg was gone. In its place was my daughter.

Beside me, Sophie gasped when she saw her gigantic double.

Haarg froze when he saw her. He knew—as we all did—that the supersize Sophie facing him in the canyon, wearing an ancient-style gown, was only an illusion. But it left Haarg vulnerable when the fake Sophie withdrew a dagger from her gown and swung it underhanded at him, sinking it into his thigh.

The real Sophie screamed.

Her giant double came after Haarg again with the dagger. He tried to knock it away with his forearm, but she was just as strong as he. She slashed him in the neck, narrowly missing his major blood vessels.

Haarg had to attack the woman he loved or be killed by her. He must overcome the natural aversion to hurting her.

"Kill her!" the real Sophie screamed.

A war god was not going to allow himself to be slaughtered without a fight. He slammed his opponent in the jaw with the pommel of his sword.

Then, imposter Sophie's dagger cleaved his forehead and nearly severed his ear.

Blood streaming into his eyes, Haarg roared and swung his sword. The dagger flew from the illusion's hand before Haarg drove his sword into her heart.

The fake Sophie dropped to her knees. Then fell face-first onto Haarg's sandaled feet.

He roared with agony at the death of his beloved.

Not so fast, big boy, I thought. Don't trust the illusion.

Haarg dropped to the ground and cradled the dying fake Sophie in his lap.

"She's not real!" Sophie shouted at him.

He did not hear her. As he stared through blood and tears at the face that looked so much like his loved one, he did not see the rest of her body, arms, and legs recede into her torso. Until her torso became a snake. He stared into what he thought were the dying eyes of his beloved while her sinuous body wrapped around his, eventually coiling around his neck.

At the last moment, as the snake constricted and squeezed the breath and life from Haarg, Sophie's fake head turned into what it really was: a serpent's head.

It opened its jaws and engulfed Haarg's face.

Sophie's shrieks in my left ear knocked me out of the illusion, revealing that no one was in the canyon anymore. Silence and emptiness filled the landscape of the In Between as the audience of gods, angels, and demons departed, leaving only we two humans atop the mesa.

The Goddess in me filled my mind with understanding.

"Haarg is not dead," I told Sophie. "Ancient gods never die; they only become irrelevant. But in this testosterone pissing match between two arrogant males, Haarg definitely lost."

"But why? He was so brave and strong."

"Wars begin with lies and end with lies. Wars kill the living while the lies never die. In other words, the Father of Lies is stronger than the God of War. As has always been the case throughout the history of humans, the Fae, and those who came before us."

"I'm glad Haarg isn't dead, but you're really bumming me out, Mom."

CHAPTER 18

THE COST OF IMMORTALITY

"I need the Goddess's assistance," said Dr. Noordlun's voice. I was in bed and thought I was dreaming. Rolling over, I suddenly found myself in the Hall of Records. Fortunately, I was fully dressed. I blinked in confusion.

"Sorry about the last-minute request," said Dr. Noordlun. He stood with his hands and forehead resting on the side of a Tugara, looking as if he were leaning against a bookcase in a library. It was kind of weird—as if I stumbled upon him doing some private ritual.

"Did I come here via astral travel? Or through a gateway? I was asleep, you see."

"A gateway brought you. I need you here physically to increase the chance the Goddess will help."

"Help with what, exactly?"

"I have been searching the archives for memories of Lethia. I've been through a good deal of her existence for over three thousand years. But I'm having difficulty reading the earliest memories of when she was human. Part of the problem is she spoke and thought in a pre-Gaelic language that is long dead. I hoped that if you channeled the Goddess, you could help me."

"But I don't know how."

"Just follow my lead and allow your instincts to take over. I'll guide you into the memories."

I mimicked Dr. Noordlun's stance and pressed my head and hands against the Tugara. At first, it felt like touching old leather-bound books, and I even caught the whiff of dusty old paper, ink, and glue. The scents were misleading because I was touching a living creature. Its thick hide felt warm. With my head resting on the creature, I soon picked up the sound of breathing and the whoosh of blood vessels.

And then whoosh—

—I was caught in the current of a river of memories. It wasn't like my psychometry when I focus on limited, concentrated psychic energy. Now, I was floating and bobbing in a flood of trillions of memories from billions of minds through millions of years.

This was the essence of the Memory Guild—what we sought, archived, and protected. The memories of everything that occurred in the world. However, in this case, it was from one Tugara's portion of the archives.

I didn't know how Dr. Noordlun could navigate through all these memories. The volume was simply overwhelming. After years of training, he could do so. And, even, bring me along for the ride.

Through the cascade of micro-images, words, sounds, scents, and emotions flowing over me like computer code, I began to pick up longer, more comprehensible scenes. Call them video clips. They were incidents taking place in a primitive village, probably in Ireland, in a very early era of civilization. I would guess it was before the Common Era, in the Iron or, even,

Bronze Age. The homes were primitive huts made with tree limbs with thatched roofs. Pigs and dogs wandered through the muddy lanes. Smoke from wood fires hung above the dwellings like fog.

Something was wrong here.

Moaning and keening by women came from nearby, and I found myself passing several fresh graves.

A disease of some sort had devastated this village. That knowledge filled my head as if it were my own memory.

Suddenly, I was inside a dimly lit hut. A fire burned low in the center of the dirt floor, smoke snaking up and out of an opening in the roof.

A woman lay on a bed with a mattress of straw. Beside her was a young girl, perhaps two years old. They looked gravely ill.

It took a while before I recognized the woman was Lethia. She was so emaciated—not at all like her powerful vampire self.

The human Lethia was muttering. At first, I thought she was babbling out of delirium. However, I realized I was hearing one side of a conversation. Was she imagining the other person? Or was it an entity not visible to me?

Like Dr. Noordlun, I did not know what she was saying. Unlike him, I have no knowledge of ancient languages. I had the Goddess, though.

The Goddess had known Lethia and these people who worshipped her and treated her like an integral part of their community. In this era, a deity wasn't an abstract concept but a character who directly affected your life.

I called upon the Goddess to assist me.

Pity and compassion surged through my heart as I looked at Lethia and her daughter. I wanted to heal them.

Of course, I wasn't really there with them.

Like a film had been removed from my eyes and ears, I suddenly comprehended everything.

"If you are a god, as you say, you can heal us," Lethia said, but not to Danu.

"I don't have the power to heal," said a male voice, the individual I couldn't see.

"Then, how will I live forever like you promise? Everyone who gets this fever dies. How can I live forever if I am dead?"

"I will bring you back to life—you and Yena. And you will never die again."

"If you have the power to do that, why can't you heal us?"

"You speak of two very different powers. Why are you not satisfied with what I promise you?"

"Because I am frightened of dying. I don't want to dwell in the Shadowlands. And what if I die and Yena lives? Who will care for her?"

"I will care for her."

"You are a god who won't show his face. You're not a mother or father."

"I am the Father of Truths."

Lethia convulsed with a coughing fit. Her young daughter moaned beside her, glistening with sweat.

Again, my Mother Goddess instincts cried out with the desire to heal them, but I was only watching a memory. It was thousands of years too late to heal Lethia and Yena.

I thought about the time when this event took place, when Danu was worshipped, and wondered why she didn't heal the village of the fever that killed so many. Why, if she couldn't intervene with the fever, did she show mercy to Lethia and give her hope after she had returned as a vampire?

The memory jumped ahead. I was in the same hut at a different time of day, with the sun low in the sky. The fire pit in the center of the floor was cold. The single room was thick with shadows.

And on the bed lay two bodies wrapped head to toe in shrouds—an adult and a child.

I did not know why I was forced to watch this memory—whose memory, exactly? There was nothing but the stillness of death.

The sun went down, and the room went dark. Still, I was stuck here watching. It occurred to me that I was waiting. And when I realized what for, I was filled with dread.

Minutes or perhaps hours later, the moon appeared, and the two shrouded bodies were tinged with silver light. I was forced to watch them and wait.

Finally, it happened. Someone moved. It was the child. She stirred slightly at first, then as she became fully conscious, she panicked and struggled to free herself from her shroud.

The cloth was soon sliced to pieces by sharp claws. And what emerged from the shroud was not a sweet child, but a monster.

Her wild eyes and frantic behavior reminded me of the infected vampires of San Marcos today.

Fangs bared, claws extended, the vampire child flung the shredded shroud from her. She sniffed the body of her mother with hunger, not affection, before realizing the dead body was of no use to her.

"This was not what I had in mind," the male voice I had heard before said. "Lethia cannot see Yena like this. It would upset her too much. She would hate me. I will take the child somewhere safe and try to tame her."

In the moonlight that seeped into the hut, a dark shadow formed, engulfing the feral vampire child. And then both the child and the shadow were gone.

Hours passed, but to me, they were mere seconds. The moon

traveled through the sky, and its silver light shifted within the hut.

The other shrouded corpse shifted, twisted, like a butterfly trying to break out of its cocoon.

A woman's voice whimpered softly. I had the urge to help her, but it was illogical because I was only a witness.

Halfway down the shrouded figure, fingers worked their way free, and soon hands emerged, followed by arms.

Lethia slowly peeled the shroud from her body and head. Though the light was dim, she didn't look any healthier than she was before her death.

I noted she behaved like one would expect: groggy, bewildered, tentative. She wasn't a savage animal like her daughter.

Was the child simply too young and formative to be brought back from death? Did the experience damage Yena's mind?

Lethia was now freed of the shroud, except where it clumped around her knees and ankles. She wrapped her arms around herself and shivered, looking at the empty fire pit.

A long, low, hopeless moan escaped her. It sounded of despair and loss.

"Where is my baby?"

The opaque, human-like shadow reappeared over her bed.

"She could not come back," said the male voice. "I am so sorry, but the child was too young to make the trip back from the Shadowlands."

Lethia sobbed.

"You, though, I brought back. You cheated death and need to fear it no more."

Lethia continued to cry. After a while, she tried to stand, but didn't have the strength.

"I'm so hungry," she said. "So weak. I don't feel alive at all."

"There is something you must know. There is a price to be

paid for coming back from death. You need to borrow the essence of life from living creatures."

"What do you mean?"

"You must feed upon their blood."

"I don't want to."

"From now on, you will be the queen of the night, the apex predator. During the day, you will hide from the sun. At night, you will reign. Only a small amount of blood you'll need to be stronger and swifter than you ever were when alive. Your existence will last forever, as long as you follow those rules."

"I don't want to live without Yena."

"Children are taken from their mothers all the time by death. You must be strong. You will have other children. Of a sort."

"I want Yena."

"I am sorry. Now, you must come with me to feed."

"There is food in the cupboard."

"You did not listen to me. No longer will you eat human food. Humans will *be* your food."

"I don't understand."

"You have been brought back from death and can hold death at bay forever. But only if you feed upon the essence of life—which is the blood of living creatures. Human blood is the best, but the blood of animals will do, if necessary."

"Before I died, you promised me eternal life."

"I never said it wouldn't have a price."

"But is this truly a life if I must hide from the sun and drink the blood of others?"

"Call it what you will. It is existence, and that's worlds better than being a shade in the Shadowlands."

"It's not better. I'll be a monster, and I won't have my daughter."

"You'll be more powerful than any human. You'll be a queen. *My* queen."

"I hate you! You lied to me."

"What is a lie? You interpret the truth differently than I."

"Go away."

"You need me to show you how to survive. Eternal existence is yours to enjoy, but not if you starve to death."

Lethia's head dropped in resignation. "I'm so hungry and weak."

"Come with me, my queen. The night will be your realm."

I stood in the Hall of Records with my forehead and hands resting on the side of the Tugara. My deep dive into the archives of memory was complete.

Dr. Noordlun stood beside me with an expectant expression. I recounted all I had learned.

"Fascinating," he said. "I wonder if her child still exists and where."

"And if she's still mentally ill. I now understand the dynamic between Lethia and the Father of Lies."

"And I question if she is truly the first vampire. I wonder if that was a lie. He spoke as if he knew other vampires."

"Maybe. I realize one thing: vampirism itself is a lie of sorts. You're not dead, but not truly alive. You depend upon the life force of others. It seems built upon a premise of untruth."

"Yes. It's why I've never been a big fan of vampires," said Dr. Noordlun. "As long as they follow the rules of society and don't prey upon me or anyone I know, I'll tolerate them. But it's like I aways say, the supernatural makes strange bedfellows. We must be their allies for mutual protection, but I'll never be their fan."

OBSERVING THE MEMORIES OF LETHIA AND THE FATHER OF Lies made me curious to know more about the demon, false god, fallen angel—whatever he truly was.

I summoned a gateway to transport me back to terrestrial earth.

"What is your name?" I asked the portal. I still had a hard time getting my head around the fact that this shimmering phenomenon was an angel.

"I am Lochlor," said a gender-neutral voice in my head.

"Please take me to Raphael." I stepped into the gateway.

I didn't know where I'd go but wasn't surprised when I arrived. My consciousness had a front-row view of the universe, facing a dark spot between distant galaxies. That dark spot was the hole in the Veil. Raphael had taken me to this vantage spot before.

"The Father of Lies was one of the original fallen angels," I said. "So, I figured you knew him."

"I did. It was no surprise he ended up the way he did. He had always been vain, dishonest, and manipulative."

I went right out and asked the question that had brought me here.

"Could he have fallen in love with a mortal? I need you to confirm what I found in the Hall of Records."

Raphael paused before saying, "Yes, he did. One reason he rebelled against God was his desire to meddle more in the affairs of humans. Well, he got his wish, and it did not go well."

"He fell in love with a mortal who died."

"Yes. As you recently learned, though he promised he would bring her back to life, what he did was bring her back as undead.

She hates him for condemning her to exist forever in that state. But, as far as I know, he still loves her, and that love motivates much of what he does, making him the cruel being he is."

"Does he have her undead daughter?"

"I have heard stories to that effect, but I do not know for sure. It is said he wanted the child as a bargaining chip, but if he reveals he has kept the child for all this time, the woman he loves will hate him even more."

"Thank you. This is valuable knowledge."

"What do you want from the Father of Lies?"

"Only to break the evil spell that has infected the vampires of my city."

"Yes. He is insecure because of his unrequited love. She is your best way to get him to break the spell."

"If I can only convince her to help me. Which won't be easy, since I can't give her what she wants from me."

CHAPTER 19

CAN'T GIVE UP HOPE

You'd think having the Goddess in me would give me a direct line to her. How I wish that were the case. Being her human incarnation works in many ways. I have the power of fecundity in me that makes my gardens flourish and tiny seedlings pop up in unexpected places. Unfortunately, it also causes weeds to thrive.

My empathy and compassion have increased. No matter how good a person you are, it's natural to get lost in your own little world at times and think of no one but yourself. Thanks to the Goddess, that happens a lot less.

And there are those rare occasions when I feel almost as if I have become the Goddess, channeling her power to both heal the hurting and destroy the perverted monsters that threaten healthy creatures.

Sometimes, I meet the Goddess face to face. While in a dreamlike state, I speak to her. It's one of the most emotionally fulfilling experiences ever.

Now, with Lethia threatening me if I don't fulfill her request,

I really, really need to speak with Danu. I'll even be satisfied with exchanging text messages, but ancient gods never respond to them.

This morning, a face appeared in my bathroom mirror. I jumped at first, afraid it was Lethia.

"A wee bit edgy, aren't ye, lass?" asked Birog.

"To be honest, yes." I explained the tough position Lethia had me in. "I need to speak directly to Danu."

"It's not as if I can help ye." The druid frowned at me, her face covered in white paint with strange runes inked on her cheeks. "Ye should be able to find the answers within yerself."

"Well, I can't. Danu gave Lethia the power of hope because she's merciful. Personally, I'd be happy to take it away, but it would go against Danu's wishes. Plus, I wouldn't know how to take it away. I want to petition her directly."

"She'll come to ye when she wishes."

"That's the problem. I've been waiting too long, and Lethia has caused serious damage. I was hoping you could use some Druid magic to summon her."

"In case ye haven't noticed, I'm just a spirit. But I'll do what I can."

She faded away from the mirror like shower steam.

So, I waited for a meeting with the Goddess. As a forgotten deity, she should have time on her hands, but apparently not. I guess I had to wait for an appointment.

A day later, the moment came at an inconvenient time. I was in the middle of serving afternoon tea.

Walking from the kitchen to the dining room, carrying a tray of freshly baked scones for the guests who were clamoring for them, I tripped on a root in a primeval forest. I didn't drop the tray, though. It simply disappeared.

So had my clothing. I was naked in the dense forest of

towering trees, a thick understory of newer growth, and a ground blanketed by ferns. Not being a naturalist, I was weirded out by being buck naked outside of the privacy of my home. In the end, though, I knew I didn't have to worry about bumping into some old perv walking his dog.

The rushing of a waterfall came to me from nearby. I knew that's where I would find Danu, as I had in the past. After all, she is also known as a water goddess, which is why the Danube River was named after her.

As I expected, I found her standing naked in a pool of water near the waterfall. Her long, black hair strategically hanging in front of her breasts.

"Hope is like water," she said to me, her words in an ancient tongue that I could somehow understand and that soothed me with its lyrical tone. "You need it to survive. Sometimes, hope flows abundantly." She gestured to the water-fall. "Sometimes, it is only a trickle. Occasionally, there is a drought of hope. That was the case with the vampire I helped."

"She doesn't want the hope anymore. She wants to destroy herself."

Danu frowned and shook her head.

"Again, hope is like water. In a drought, everyone suffers. If I take hope away from one person, its absence will hurt those around her. An entire tribe could die if they all lose hope and the will to live. When you catch a school of minnows and put them in a bucket, if some die, it causes them all to die from the stress of it."

She smiled at me as if I completely understood her meaning.

"Hope is not an individual's choice," she continued. "It is a way of life. I cannot take it away from one person without harming all of those around her."

"She's surrounded by vampires who don't have good intentions."

"The vampires that lived among you before had good intentions, because they had hope that if they didn't cause harm, they could live in peace."

"So, you're saying you won't grant Lethia's request?"

"I shall not. Without hope, she has nowhere to go but the abyss. With hope, she'll find other ways. Perhaps, even the path to redemption."

"I don't know. She is punishing me for not giving her—"

"Clotted cream and jam, please," said the table of elderly ladies where I stood with my tray of scones.

"Of course," I said, happy to grant the request.

Unlike the stubborn deity within me.

MISSY SAT ON THE FLOOR OF THE INN'S KITCHEN, INSIDE A magic circle. She was performing her locator spell with Bob's beaded necklace that had broken off his neck when he crawled through the bathroom window of the auto repair shop.

"The orb of his spirit essence can't find him." She shook her head sadly. "I'm afraid that means he's dead."

Sophie and I gasped.

"I'm sorry—I meant undead. I think he's already been turned, and it changed his psychic energy. This necklace was last worn by him when he was human."

"That's so unfair," Sophie said. "Why Bob? He's critically important to the guilds."

"You answered your own question," I said. "Lethia took him to decapitate the guilds. Who is going to take over as the head of the Magic Guild now?"

"Baldric wants the position, but some members are against it because he's a faerie and practices different magic than most of them. A wizard named Orlena has my vote."

Missy wiped away a section of her circle to break the spell. She extinguished the five candles and got wearily to her feet.

"If Bob has been turned, he'll be beholden to Lethia, of course. But he was too powerful a mage for his spirit to be completely broken. He'll probably need to relearn his magic now that he's no longer human, but we might be able to convince him to fight back against Lethia. He could be our spy on the inside."

"If we can find him," I said.

"If Bob is still Bob, you know where we'll eventually find him," said Sophie.

She was right. Once he adjusted to his new identity, he would surely return to surfing—although under the stars instead of the sun.

We took turns each night going to the beach to look for him, to no avail. It was risky going out at night with both the infected vampires and Lethia's followers out hunting. Being members of guilds made us especially vulnerable to be targeted for attack.

We always travelled in twos: Missy with Cory, and Sophie with me, so a witch casting protection spells would always be there. We each wore so many anti-vampire amulets that we looked like tourists laden with beads at Mardi Gras.

On nights when there was no surf, we stayed home. But on every night with decent waves, we traveled to the beach. It was impossible to see all the coastline from the road, since in many cases, homes and condo buildings blocked the view. So, we would have to find a place to park, trek through the dunes, and look up and down the beach for a lone surfer, before returning to our car, driving a few miles, and parking again.

Of course, we always started at the public beaches where Bob used to surf, but I suspected he would find more remote spots now. With a vampire's ability to run long distances quickly, he wouldn't need his jeep, which would have been easy to find parked along A1A.

Finally, on a night with a nearly full moon, Sophie and I spotted someone paddling a surfboard out past the breakers. It was a cool night, but the person wasn't wearing a wetsuit. And when he stood on his board, the bulging gut gave him away.

It was Bob.

"You'd think being on a liquid diet, he would lose some weight," I said.

"Mom! Don't talk like that."

I shrugged. She was right—I was being catty. Besides, we were here to win him over, not criticize.

We stood on the beach and watched him ride the waves. As he finished, he saw us and walked ashore carrying his board.

Would he be friendly or hostile? Would he attack? Sophie cast a protection spell around us, just in case.

"Yo, dudes," he said, dripping with water. "What's up?"

He was being polite, but he didn't seem to recognize us. He sniffed, trying to read our scents. You'd think that would be strictly werewolf behavior, but vampires also have remarkably sensitive olfactory glands.

"It's Darla and Sophie," Sophie said. "Don't you recognize us?"

"You look familiar."

"You tutored me in magic. Don't you remember?"

"I've gone through some big changes lately."

"That's why we're here—to see how you're doing," I said. "We've been very worried about you."

He squeezed water from his shaggy blond hair and looked away from us, at the moon's reflection upon the ocean.

"I've felt, like, pretty gnarly. Only in the past day or so, I've been a little better."

Sophie spoke up. "You were, um. . ."

"Turned? Yes. By Lethia. My existence will never be the same. It's kind of a bummer. The good thing is, I'll never grow too old to surf."

"Yeah, you've got that going for you," I said.

"Okay, I remember you dudes now. It's coming back to me. Pieces of me are still missing, but lots of stuff has returned. I've been coming into the surf shop at night. Haven't found a way yet to explain to my employees why I can't come in during the day."

"They don't need to know. You're the boss."

"Do you think I can still be the leader of the Magic Guild?"

Sophie and I exchanged glances.

"That's up to the guild to decide," Sophie said.

"Yeah, Lethia probably wouldn't let me do it, anyway. She's under orders to destroy the guilds."

"How do you feel about that?" I asked.

He shrugged. "It's my maker's wish."

"No, it's the wish of the Father of Lies."

"Doesn't matter. I have to obey her."

"It *does* matter. She's following his orders because he is her maker. But she hates him."

"Doesn't matter."

"Listen to me, Bob. I know you don't like being subservient to Lethia."

"I have no choice."

"Yes, you do. Most vampires aren't slaves to their makers. We need to convince Lethia to leave San Marcos and not destroy the guilds. She's going to attack too many humans and attract the authorities' attention. And then you'll all be staked. You don't want that, do you?"

"No way."

"We need you to help us turn Lethia against The Father of Lies. He's the one who's pushing her to go too far."

"How am I supposed to do that? I don't even know the dude."

"You know him indirectly. He's responsible for a lot of the world's problems."

"I'm one of Lethia's newest children. She won't listen to me."

"You were one of the most powerful magicians in the South-east," Sophie said. "You were a role model for me. I don't think I would have become a water witch if it weren't for you."

His face dropped with sadness. "I'm not powerful anymore. My magic is all messed up now. I couldn't cast a spell if the world depended on it."

"You'll re-learn your craft. I know you will," Sophie said. "Imagine how powerful you'll be. You'll probably be the only mage vampire."

"I'd have to get Lethia's permission to re-learn my craft."

"Nonsense," I said. "Just go ahead and do it. She has too many followers to keep close watch on you."

He scratched his head. "It would feel awesome to do magic again."

"You can use it to influence Lethia," I said.

"Let's not go too far," he said, looking frightened.

He stepped away from us. His fear must have triggered something primal in him because he was as tight as a piano wire and looked at us like he'd forgotten again who we were.

He turned his head slightly, and the moon caught his face. His pupils were enlarged, and a yellow glow came from the whites of his eyes.

I touched Sophie's arm. She glanced at me and saw how I was

looking at Bob. Her lips moved as she strengthened the protection spell around us.

"You're using a protection spell," he said. "The old me would have noticed right away instead of taking this long."

"No worries," Sophie said. "You have a lot on your mind."

"Yes. Like feeding. Riding the waves works up an appetite."

Frankly, I was tired of dealing with newly turned vampires and their lack of self-control.

"Don't even think about feeding on us," I said, as if what I said would make a difference.

Because once a vampire thinks about feeding on you, it's already too late.

Bob took a step toward us. He hesitated, part of him fighting the urges he did not fully understand.

"Bob! Knock it off. We're friends."

Sophie and I backed away slowly from him. Any sudden movements would get us killed.

"I wish I had my sword," Sophie whispered.

"You can't bring your sword everywhere. You need an enchanted dagger. It's more portable and—"

I tripped over a formation of coquina protruding from the sand.

Bob shot toward us like a rattlesnake and bounced off the shield of the protection spell.

Bob's gift was magic. Without it, he was just a lumbering, overweight, middle-aged man who retained some of his surfing talent. The problem was a lumbering middle-aged guy who was a vampire posed a major threat.

Sophie helped me to my feet. Speaking of lumbering middle-aged people.

Bob warily circled us like a wolf, looking for an opening to attack.

"Bob, please remember who you are," Sophie said. "You're a friend and mentor."

He was long past reasoning. Somehow, we had to make it to the car, start it, and get out of here without him finding a way into our bubble of protection.

We kept moving toward the dunes, and Bob kept circling us, looking more limber and less lumbering with each pass.

"Do you have anything stronger, even without your sword?" I asked Sophie. "What about a sleeping spell?"

Sophie scoffed. "I prefer attack spells, not sweet little lullabies."

"I don't care what you use, as long as it stops him."

Sophie stopped and knelt beside another outcropping of coquina. A basin-like formation at the bottom still held seawater from when the earlier high tide had covered these rocks. She placed both hands in the little pool of water, which was the size of a soup bowl.

The water turned purple and crackled with electricity. The magic had turned it solid, and Sophie lifted the disc from the rock.

She tossed the spinning disc at Bob. It passed through our protection bubble and hit him squarely in the gut. He screamed as he became engulfed in purple static.

"Run!" Sophie commanded.

She ran, I lumbered. We made it over the dunes and almost to the side of the road where our car was parked.

But Bob was in front of us, blocking our path.

"How did you get here?" I asked, not expecting an answer.

Bob was clearly out of his mind. His face had the most unusual expression, and I barely recognized him.

"You see what I have done?" A woman's voice came from his mouth. It was Lethia's. "I turned the most powerful magician in

San Marcos into my little boy toy. And he is just the beginning."
His eyes turned to me, but the voice was still hers. "When will
you grant my request?"

"Um, the Goddess isn't too keen on the idea of taking away
hope."

"You are the Goddess incarnate. You have your own will and
can do what I ask. After all, you will pay the price if you don't."

"But I can't."

"You haven't even tried. Free me from this hope."

"Really, I can't. I don't even know how I could do it."

"Not only will I destroy all the guilds, but I will also make
you suffer the consequences personally. Someone near and dear
to you will become my next slave unless you grant my request."

I looked at Sophie. Her face had gone almost as white as
Bob's.

"Cast all the spells you want, but I will come to your home
soon," Lethia's voice said. "You will do as I say, or I will take your
loved one."

Bob came out of whatever spell she had possessed him with.
He fell to his knees and covered his face. His blood lust seemed
to have left him.

"Go," he said in his own voice. "Get out of here before the
hunger takes me over again."

We ran past him to the car. He was sobbing heavily as we
drove away.

CHAPTER 20
BATTLE MAGIC

A witches' conference was going on in the inn's living room that evening. Sophie and Missy sat on the couch facing a diminutive African-American woman in a wingback chair. The three women sipped tea and talked magic.

"Actually, I know several battle spells that use benevolent elemental magic," the woman said. She appeared to be in her sixties, with braided gray hair and twinkling eyes.

"I've always used magic to heal and to protect," Missy said.

"To heal, you must fight germs and disease," the woman said.

Sophie noticed me standing in the doorway.

"Mom, I'd like you to meet Orlena."

I approached Orlena and shook her tiny hand.

"Welcome to the Esperanza Inn," I said.

"Your inn has such a lovely name: hope."

"Sometimes, the name is too on-the-nose," I said, even though it was a bit of sarcasm no one else would get except for a certain vampire.

"Orlena is a very accomplished wizard," Sophie explained.

"We met through the Magic Guild. She's teaching me new spells."

"Your daughter has great potential as a witch. She's very interested in battle spells."

"Oh, yes. That's for sure."

"I'm teaching Sophie how to defeat an opponent without using brute force. Sort of like judo or jujitsu with magic."

"She uses magic that draws from your opponent's strength and uses it against them," Sophie said. "Let's show Mom what we're working on."

Sophie pulled her sword from beneath the sofa. I instinctively glanced around to make sure no guests were nearby. A sword makes a great decoration in an old inn, but it's weird to use it for anything else.

Sophie stood about ten feet away from Orlena, gripped her sword with two hands, and aimed it at the wizard.

"I'm going to do an energy burst like I use against the vampires. But at much lower power."

She murmured words I couldn't make out, and the steel of her sword glowed with a purple light. Then, a familiar bolt of what looked like lightning arced from the blade and shot toward Orlena's face.

I gasped. This purple lighting has destroyed many a vampire and turned anthropophagi into volcanoes of goo.

Orlena calmly crossed her arms at the wrists, her palms flat, and caught the lightning. It bounced right off her wrists and hit Sophie's sword, knocking it from her hands.

"Ouch," Sophie said.

"Sorry. You should have used less power."

"Quite impressive," I said.

"That's only one very obvious example of what I'm talking about," said Orlena. "It's about more than turning your opponent's weapon against her. There are more subtle ways to use the technique, such as harvesting your enemy's psychic energy."

"I've been talking to Diego about what makes Lethia such a powerful vampire," Sophie said. "The power doesn't come from magic forces. It has something to do with death. I want to figure out how to use it to destroy her."

That's my girl. Brilliant, brave, and ballsy.

"What do you think of this approach, Missy?" I asked.

"It suits my style better than harnessing my own power to hurt someone. With my background as a nurse, I guess I'll always be more of a pacifist."

"As should most witches," Sophie said. "Some witches, though, have to fight bad guys. I guess that's my career path."

Too bad it doesn't come with a great salary and benefits.

AFTER THE WITCHES LEFT, I MADE FINAL ROUNDS OF THE INN. It was an old habit of mine, taking a last look around before retiring for the night, just to make sure all was well. Of course, I wouldn't know if there was a problem behind my guests' doors. Still, I needed the peace-of-mind that no accident was waiting to happen in the common areas.

Beginning upstairs, I made my way down to the ground floor. I checked the exterior doors to make sure they were locked. After 7 p.m., guests needed a keycard to enter. If you were a late-arriving new guest, you had to ring the buzzer at the main door for an innkeeper to let you in.

All was as it should be. Except for the fact that audio was coming from the television in the living room. I rarely turned it on, because it didn't fit in with the 300-year-old vibe here, but sometimes guests like to gather to watch important sports events.

Sophie was still in here, and Haarg had shown up. They sat close together on the couch as Haarg listlessly changed channels with the remote, just like a human male. I was relieved to see Haarg also appeared in the form of a normal human male wearing normal clothing in case a guest saw him.

"You must get over it, my lord," Sophie said.

She called him "my lord"? Yeah, he was a god, but you'd never catch me calling a boyfriend "my lord."

"It was humiliating," he replied. "I will get vengeance."

"Are you talking about your battle with Aastacki?" I asked. "It wasn't a fight to the death, so it was no big deal. You'll challenge him to another fight some other time."

"I was defeated in front of my love. And her mother. It was a disgrace."

"I'm just happy you weren't permanently hurt," Sophie said.

"He disguised himself as you. It threw me off my game."

"Aastacki is a liar and a trickster," I said. "He has no honor."

"He should be slain."

"Yeah!" agreed Sophie. I swear, she has become enamored with slaying.

After all the channel changing, Haarg had alighted on cable news. I happened to catch the caption crawling along the bottom of the screen. There was something about missiles fired in the Middle East.

Haarg, staring at the screen, had a smug grin.

"Wait," I said. "Did you have anything to do with that missile attack?"

"I do not fire missiles."

"I mean, did you influence the humans who did it?"

He shrugged. "I am the God of War. That's what I do."

189

Of course, I knew that. But to see him in action, casually sparking hostilities in an already tense conflict, made me angry.

"You're a Fae god. Why are you messing with humans?"

"I mess with everyone. All you intelligent hominids love war. I just nudge you in the direction you were already going."

"I think that's despicable."

"Mom!" Sophie scolded.

"Your politicians do it more often than I do," Haarg replied. "And for more despicable reasons."

"You did it just now because you're bored and in a bad mood."

He raised his eyebrows mockingly. "You're certain of that? You don't believe I have grand strategic reasons for spurring the attack?"

"No."

"You're right!" He laughed uproariously, slapping his knee.

I frowned at him.

"I thought I was earning your affection," he said.

"It will always be an uphill battle for you. As I told you before, I represent a goddess of birth and healing. You're the opposite of that."

"Let me get one thing clear, Darla—"

"Mrs. Chesswick."

"When I was here for dinner, you said I could call you Darla."

"You can call me Darla only when I'm not mad at you."

"Mrs. Chesswick, in the worlds of humans, Fae, elves, trolls, pixies—the lot of you—there will always be conflict over land and resources. That is not my fault. What I do is elevate war into an art form. I make it glorious."

"In the eyes of bards and propagandists."

"Yes, everyone who sings of war. Your species need me to

make war seem glorious. Otherwise, you'd all fall into despair at the misery you cause—if I existed or not. I make it easier for your species to live with yourselves when you do things that are, well, despicable."

"We shouldn't be doing them at all."

"But you will. You always have and you always will."

Maybe he was right, but it seemed too cynical to believe that. I dream of a world without suffering, death, and destruction caused by those who live in it. With the Goddess inside of me, I wish for it even more fervently.

But will such a world ever exist? I doubted it, but I will never stop hoping for it.

Which brings me to Haarg. Can I really endure having this god as a son-in-law?

"Haarg," Sophie said. "Enough of the shop talk. You can fight Aastacki some other time. Tonight, let's talk about me."

Can a god really endure a wife as strong headed as my daughter?

WHEN A VAMPIRE VOWS TO COME AFTER A LOVED ONE, YOU take it seriously. Most families would leave town. Heck, I wanted to leave the country. But we couldn't. We had an inn to run, and you can't hire a temp to handle your family business.

In Florida, we overuse the expression "hunker down," which refers to putting up your hurricane shutters and taking shelter inside with your battery-operated lanterns until the storm passes. I hate the expression, but it aptly describes our strategy while waiting for a vampire attack.

As usual, our marketing ingenuity failed to get all our rooms booked, so Cory and I moved from our vulnerable cottage in the courtyard to the room next to Sophie's. Missy stayed in the room next door. We also gave a vacant room on the second floor to Diego, so we would have another vampire onsite. Diego and we four humans were on a group text in case we needed to call for help.

Roderick would prowl the building's exterior, while Archibald would serve as our sentinel gargoyle.

The humans were covered in amulets and armed with sharpened wooden stakes. The inn was saturated with warding and protection spells.

Of course, the inn had an electronic security system, but would you really trust that to keep out a vampire?

So, we were as ready as we could be. We even took turns standing watch throughout the night. The problem was, Lethia didn't show up—not on the first night, nor the second. The anxiety and lack of sleep were weighing on us.

The only time we could relax was during the day. We did a lot of napping, neglecting maintenance work and other chores.

It was Tuesday afternoon. Cory and I surprised each other with a spontaneous lovemaking session, then curled up for a nice long nap before I had to prepare the afternoon tea. The heavy curtains were closed, the room was dark, and I went out like a light.

My dreams were mundane at first. Then, they became vivid. I stood naked on the rocky outcropping of a cliff, the tops of trees below me. A vast forest spread for as far as I could see, with pockets of mist hovering over parts of it. Behind me was a great river.

I was Danu, the earth-mother goddess who watched over this pristine land.

"Take back your gift, Danu."

The words were a woman's, and they weren't humble and imploring. They were demanding.

"It is not graceful to refuse a gift," I said.

"I don't want it. This is the last time I will ask you."

A hint of a snarl came at the end. My eyes shot open. I wasn't Danu—I was Darla, lying in the bed of 304.

And Lethia's face was inches from mine.

"This is your last chance." She had horrible breath that reeked of death and rot.

I don't know why I was distracted by her halitosis, but it sure woke me up.

Her hands clamped down on the comforter, trapping mine. My heart took off in triple time.

"Hope—be gone from this woman." It sounded stupid, but it was all I could think to say. I reached inside of myself to encourage the heat that meant the Goddess was possessing me. But there was no heat, only icy fear.

"You're not even trying," Lethia scoffed.

Suddenly, my arms were free, and she was on the other side of the bed, leaning over Cory.

She bared her fangs.

"Please, Danu, free Lethia of the hope that blinds her. Please!"

Nothing burned within me. Nothing changed.

Before I could say another word, Lethia opened her mouth so wide her jaw dislocated, and she chomped down on Cory's neck.

His eyes opened, but they were unfocused as sucking sounds filled the room.

"No!" I shouted as I scrambled across the bed and pushed Lethia away. But she didn't move. Her backhand struck my cheek, and I landed on the floor.

My phone was on the bedside table. I crawled to it and opened the group text.

"Hel" was all my panicked fingers sent, but everyone would know I was in trouble.

Why was Lethia here in the daytime? Was she that powerful? How did she even get here while avoiding the sun? Did she have one of those cars with the illegally tinted windows?

The wooden stakes were propped up by the door. But I had a better idea. While Lethia guzzled Cory's blood, I rushed past the bed to the window to yank the curtains.

I dropped to the floor, paralyzed. Lethia had mesmerized me.

The door rattled. Man, I wish it wasn't locked, but, you know, Cory and I had been occupied.

Sophie has a passkey, though. A few minutes later, the door opened softly.

Sophie and Missy peered into the room with horror.

I was too mesmerized to talk. I could only lie on the floor staring at my daughter and cousin helplessly, while the fiend slurped my husband's lifeblood.

The door burst fully open. Sophie stood there, sword in hand.

"Stop it, you foul creature!" she cried.

The purple bolts shot from the sword, hitting Lethia but having no effect.

"Use Orlena's method," Missy whispered.

"But I don't know how to harness her powers. I don't understand them."

"Vampires don't just drink blood for its nutritional value. The blood carries a bit of the soul that animates you—the life force that keeps you alive. That's how they cheat death."

Sophie squinted her eyes in frustration as she tried to figure out how to exploit what Missy had said.

"Draw the life force from the blood in her stomach. Steal it from her and give it back to Cory."

Sophie's face relaxed, and she nodded. She pointed her sword at Lethia and got closer. The vampire looked up, her face crimson with blood. It looked like she was trying to mesmerize Sophie, but my daughter and Missy must have cast warding spells to protect themselves.

Sophie closed her eyes. Her lips moved soundlessly. Then, the strangest thing happened.

White light flowed not from the sword, but *toward* it. It came from Lethia, crackling across the air before it met the sword's point.

The sword glowed white. Sophie's hair stood on end.

Lethia moaned and fell away from the bed, landing on the floor before scrambling to her feet. She hissed like a cornered cat.

The transfer of energy stopped, and the sword lost its glow.

"You can't stop me or hurt me, foolish witches. I will be back to finish draining this stupid human. And take all of you, as well."

She faded away and disappeared, like she had when she invaded the bathroom recently.

"Return the life force to Cory," Missy said.

Sophie seemed unclear how to do it, but she approached the bed and lay the flat of the sword's blade on Cory's head.

The sword glowed white again, and so did Cory, as if he had a halo around his head.

He looked a little better than he had when Lethia released him. He had seemed anemic to the point of death. Now, he had a fighting chance.

"Can we call nine-one-one?" Missy asked. "I might be able to get my hands on some plasma, but he needs a transfusion at a hospital."

The unstated truth was that he had two raw puncture marks on his neck. How would we explain them to paramedics and law enforcement?

But there was no way I'd put his health in jeopardy to maintain this supernatural omertà.

I can't control the Goddess's powers enough to keep Cory out of the hospital. But I believed I could heal him enough to make it look like he had a household injury rather than a vampire attack.

Holding my hand against his wounds, I felt the burning within me and the power flow from my hands into his wounds.

Where was this power when I needed it to get Lethia off our backs?

There was a brief sizzling sound where my hand touched his neck. I pulled it away, and there was now a smaller wound that didn't look like it was caused by punctures.

It also didn't look like it would cause the severe blood loss Cory suffered. But it would have to do.

"Let me call Detective Samson and tip him off about what happened. He can help sanitize the incident report," I said.

I gave him the basic information. Neither he nor I were alone, so I couldn't elaborate. But when the ambulance arrived, I was confident that no strange questions would arise.

I rode with Cory in the ambulance. At the hospital, the transfusion made a tremendous difference. The ER doctor was surprised by the amount of antibiotics Cory needed. I couldn't explain it was because of a vampire bite. It had been a shaving accident, I lied. Missy, who met me at the hospital, said vampire saliva reduces infections and aids healing, so victims will be in good shape for future feedings. Lethia, however, was a more primitive kind of vampire because of her age.

"She's going to return," I said to Missy while Cory slept. "Sophie's magic is more effective now, but we can't count on it stopping Lethia."

"You have a plan in mind. I can tell from the look in your eyes."

"Yes. You and I are making a little outing to the In Between."
"What? Why?"

"Because I believe the only thing that will stop Lethia will be finding her daughter. And I'm guessing her daughter is being hidden in the In Between."

CHAPTER 21
BETWEEN A ROCK AND A
HIDING PLACE

Missy was one of the few people I knew who had been to the In Between, Cory being another. Witches and other magicians traveled there to escape persecution on earth. I met a witch there once who had fled the Salem witch trials.

I knew of no vampires who went to the In Between, probably because the gateways refused to take them. Gods and demons of various sorts could go there without the help of gateways.

My guess is that the Father of Lies took Yena there to hide her from Lethia. It was the only place imaginable where Lethia would never find her, and no witnesses would report to Lethia of having seen her.

"How will *we* find her?" Missy asked when I proposed the journey. "I don't think anyone can navigate that place."

She was right. The In Between was a vast alternate plane of existence with a diverse topography that was ever changing. I'd been dropped off and picked up in locations not of my choosing, but I never journeyed from place to place on my own without a human guide.

"If she is there, she would need blood to survive," I said. "As a toddler, she probably can't hunt very well on her own—even with her vampire speed and strength. Besides, her state of mind is like a rabid animal. The Father of Lies probably brings her victims to feed upon."

"There are so few humans in the In Between that they would know about a toddler vampire preying upon them."

"And would stake her. It's just a guess, but I would bet The Father of Lies abducts people from earth to bring to her, then returns them."

"If that's the case, she could be hidden away, and we'll never find her."

"Don't despair, cousin. We have angels to help us."

You can't find anything to eat or drink in the In Between unless you can create it with magic. Missy said she didn't know how to do that. So, we each wore a small backpack filled with water bottles and granola bars. Missy carried magic supplies, and I brought a heavy-duty plastic leaf bag and duct tape. I'd found that you can bring objects to the In Between as long as they're on your body.

Sophie was in charge of protecting Cory while we were gone. The odd thing about the In Between is that you can spend hours or days there but be missing from earth for only a few seconds. So, I wasn't too worried about leaving Cory.

When we were ready, I summoned a gateway. Before we stepped into it, I asked it its name. Thanks to the Goddess in me, the gateways were always amenable.

"I am Uriel."

"Do you know if the Father of Lies visits the In Between?"

"Yes. I have seen him before."

"Does he bring humans there?"

"I don't know, but it's very possible."

"Where have you seen him? That's where we want to go."

"Are you sure? It is a very rugged and remote place."

"Are there any human encampments nearby?"

"Yes, there is one."

"Please take us there."

"And don't forget about us," Missy added. "We'll need a ride home. Thanks!"

With a lurch of my stomach, we stepped through the portal I used to nickname the Barf Bus before I learned gateways were angels.

As usual, we didn't have a smooth landing. Missy and I tumbled onto the grass of a small meadow. I picked myself up and looked around.

The meadow was next to a gigantic forest. Above us was a mountain with a rocky cliff jutting out over the forest. It reminded me of my most recent vision of the Goddess in my dream. Was she giving me a clue of where to search?

At the far edge of the meadow, before the trees began again, was a wisp of smoke from a campfire. It wasn't an actual fire, of course, only magic. A cluster of small wooden huts surrounded it. We walked toward it, hoping the people we met were friendly.

A wizened old man wearing a monk's habit emerged from a hut and walked toward us. He carried a staff. The humans I'd met here used tools like that to fight the strange monsters who also lived in the In Between.

He greeted us speaking a language that I couldn't place. Some words sounded vaguely like English, while others were like French.

We raised our hands and smiled at him, nodding dumbly.

"I have a translation spell," Missy whispered to me. "Give me a moment."

She pulled a vial from her backpack and opened it. She poured a few drops of liquid in one hand, then rubbed it into her ears. Then she took a small sip and grimaced. Replacing the vial, she recited a spell.

The man watched her with interest, then spoke to us again in the tone of a question.

"Ah, it's Middle English," Missy whispered to me. "The language of Chaucer."

"Who's Chaucer?"

"Never mind."

She spoke to him in the same language. It was odd hearing it come from Missy's mouth. She asked him several questions, which he answered.

Then, he pointed to the rocky cliff and spoke in a fearful tone.

"I told him we were looking for a vampire child," Missy said to me. "He didn't seem to think that was unusual at all. I guess in his era, England was abundant with supernatural creatures."

"That was when Archibald was created," I said. "Remind me to never time travel there."

"He said he's never seen the Father of Lies, but he has heard people screaming up on the mountain at night from time to time. Once, two refugees camping here hiked up there to investigate and never came back. Since then, no one will go near the place."

"It sounds like we've found the right location."

"Yeah." Missy looked up at the cliff nervously. "Is this really such a good idea?"

"It's the only plan I can think of, other than allowing Lethia to turn Cory and defeat all of us. Ask the monk if he will go with us part of the way, so we don't get lost or attacked by some strange creature."

Missy spoke to him. He seemed hesitant. There was some back and forth before he finally nodded.

I'd never been in the In Between at night, and I didn't know how long the days lasted. We embarked on our hike right away to avoid being on the mountain when the vampire was active.

We followed the monk across the meadow and through the trees. There was no trail; the monk took a route between the larger pine trees. Oddly, the ground was not carpeted in pine needles—just another reminder that the In Between was not what it appeared to be.

Missy walked as close to the monk as she could and tried to engage him in conversation. He obviously didn't follow a vow of silence but was not very gregarious. His face was weathered and stern, but the dark-brown hair around his tonsure lacked any gray, so I guessed he was younger than he looked.

After a while, Missy dropped back and filled me in.

"His name is Celric, and he comes from a long line of mages. When the churches of his diocese cracked down hard on witch-craft, he entered a monastery, hoping to leave magic behind. But it was too much in his blood. He couldn't avoid doing magical things. So, he was forced to leave the monastery. He follows the monastic life here, returning to earth only when necessary to rebuild his health after spending time here."

Being in this alternate plane of existence, where everything is an illusion, creates molecular deterioration in mammals. It seems not to bother dragons too much, because they spend much longer periods here than humans can.

I grew tired of walking.

"How much farther are we going? It shouldn't be this far if they can hear the screams of Yena's victims."

"It's the topography that lets sound travel further. The meadow is in a sort of bowl between the mountain and the forest. And we're taking a roundabout route to come up the other side of the cliff."

Properly schooled, I kept my mouth shut.

For about five minutes. Until I screamed.

"Are you freaking serious?" I cried.

A squirrel was barreling towards us in attack mode. No, not a cute squirrel—this guy was as big as a grizzly bear, and his tail was longer than my car.

"Oh, my," said Missy.

The giant rodent seemed to come specifically for me. I tried to engage the Goddess's powers to tell this guy not to eat his nature deity, but I remembered he wasn't an actual living creature. He was a magical construct, capable of tearing me to pieces without being hungry.

Celric ran to get between the squirrel and me. He swung his staff at the beast but missed. The squirrel leaped to a tree trunk, and then over Celric, knocking the monk down with its giant bushy tail.

I slipped behind a large tree trunk and pulled out a granola bar, holding it toward the squirrel. Yeah, right. He was going to pass up a delicious human for a sensible snack.

The squirrel reached my tree and instinctively jumped onto the trunk, hanging on by its claws, and crawled around it to get to me.

I scurried around the trunk, staying just out of reach of its mouth.

The squirrel, frustrated, climbed higher and tried to get me from above. I ran behind the neighboring tree.

The monster squirrel jumped, soaring right toward me.

Before exploding in a spray of black smoke as the monk's staff hit it.

There was no blood or goo—only smoke, as the illusion was destroyed.

"Could he really have killed me?" I asked. Missy translated.

The monk nodded and said, "*Yis*," which was close enough to "yes" for me to feel unsteady on my feet.

The monk spoke some more.

"He says many of the creatures of the In Between are deadly, he believes, to discourage living humans and other intelligent species from coming here. The In Between is really meant to be a way station for souls on their ways to Heaven or Hell."

"I know. And for foolish people like us."

WE SOON REACHED THE TOP OF THE CLIFF OVERLOOKING THE valley. Behind it, the slope of the mountain continued to rise as the trees' growth fell away. From this angle, I could see around the side of the mountain to a deeper valley where a mighty river flowed.

This setting was so similar to the one in my dream of the Goddess. She must have been sending a message to me.

We walked on the flat area of rock that led to the cliff, and a dark opening came into view.

"No, not a cave," I said. "I don't want to go into a cave."

We reached it and peered inside.

"No, especially not a cave with bloodstains on the rocks."

Missy shrugged. "What did you expect? A cute little vampire sitting in a stroller that we could wheel home?"

My sarcasm was rubbing off on her. I needed to focus on the matter at hand.

"Okay, Missy, your immobility and sleep spells will be key to restraining her while I bind her with the tape. We'll cover her with the leaf bag to protect her from light when we take her from the cave. If she wakes up down there in the darkness, she's going to be a little tiger. Your magic must work."

"Thanks for adding pressure."

"Are you ready?"

She nodded. The monk made the sign of the cross. That reminded me to pull the cross I was wearing around my neck out from under my blouse.

The cave was barely big enough for us to squeeze in one by one. Based on the bloodstains outside, the Father of Lies brought humans to the cave mouth and restrained them while Yena crawled out to feed upon them.

Missy recited her incantations in the darkness as she slipped around a rock wall in front of me. She gasped and stopped suddenly. I collided with her back.

A growl like from an angry kitten chilled me to the bone. It cut off.

Missy moved ahead, and we entered a small chamber. Missy created an illumination orb revealing a cot and a cute little feral vampire toddler. Remembering how much attitude Sophie had when she was a toddler, I couldn't imagine how vicious this one was.

Fortunately, Yena lay perfectly still, sleeping heavily. Missy's spells had worked.

I bound the little monster with duct tape Missy had enchanted for extra strength. Next, I wrapped the leaf bag over her for her protection.

She was lighter than I had imagined as I carried her from the cave.

Celric stepped away from me in fear. The leaf bag must have been emitting seriously scary vibes.

Missy thanked him profusely for his help, and I summoned a gateway to take us home.

Now, the tricky part would be how to reunite Lethia with her daughter in a way that made her grateful enough to help us against the Father of Lies.

And to not kill us.

CHAPTER 22

BAG OF WOLVERINES

I know, I told you that when you take a trip to the In Between, no matter how long it takes, you're away from earth for only seconds. Well, I was wrong. This trip lasted thousands of seconds for some unknown reason.

So, somehow, we returned to the inn during Teatime. It was a bit awkward. Missy's spells were wearing off already, which meant carrying Yena was like carrying a bag full of fighting wolverines. And we reappeared right in the middle of the foyer.

The hideous growling and whining caused all the heads in the dining room to look our way. The thrashing vampire toddler threatened to burst through the leaf bag at any moment.

Sophie, who was handling the tea service, glared at us and jerked her head in a get-out-of-here manner.

"Let's go to the utility room," I whispered to Missy.

The leaf bag growled and jerked.

"How are we going to keep her from eating our faces?" Missy asked as we hurried down the hall. "My spells wore off way too quickly."

"Traveling from the In Between probably messed up the magic. You'll need to cast the spells again."

The elevator dinged as we approached it on our way down the hall. Two people stepped into our path.

It was Debbie and a young dude with a tattooed head.

"This is the owner," she said to him. "She turned my uncle into a vampire."

"I did not! I bear no liability for it."

"If you admit that he's a vampire, I can make you internet-famous," the man said.

"Rolph is a social media influencer known for his occult videos," Debbie explained. "He's going to help me document Uncle Hendrik's vampirism for any future legal action. If we can find my uncle again."

"I know nothing about vampires," I lied. "I don't even believe in them."

An ear-splitting shriek came from the leaf bag and a knee knocked me in the back of the head.

"What's in that bag?" Debbie asked.

"A cat—"

"A dog—" Missy and I spoke over each other.

Rolph pulled out his phone to capture video.

"Which is it?" Debbie demanded.

"It's kind of a hybrid. A cat-dog-wolverine. We're taking it to animal control right now. Did I mention it's rabid?"

"Here in a notorious haunted inn, vampires have been known to lurk," narrated Rolph for his video.

"This inn is *not* notorious," I said.

"We need to go to Animal Control *now*," Missy said.

"And what's this talk about legal action? The inn accepts no liability for vampire attacks."

"You admit Uncle Hendrik was attacked by a vampire?" Debbie asked.

"Not here. I mean, no. I don't believe in vampires."

The cat-dog-wolverine whined and thrashed again.

"Is the creature in that bag supernatural?" Rolph asked.

"It's just ill-tempered," I said. "Please let us get past you so we can get this creature some compassionate care."

I was afraid Yena would burst through the bag, be exposed to sunlight, and go up in smoke. A vampire was bad enough. Destroying one who was a minor would get me into all sorts of trouble.

I needed a distraction.

"Hey, how would you like to capture video of an almost guaranteed ghost experience?"

"Where?" Rolph asked.

"In this inn. I disagree that the inn is notorious, but it *is* haunted. The most dependable ghost is Elvis."

"Elvis Presley?" both Debbie and Rolph asked in disbelief.

"Actually, Virgil Bungcroft. But he was an Elvis impersonator. Good one, too. He croaked in the hot tub of Room 202. The room isn't booked right now, so you can go up there and set up a camera. Even if you don't see him, you'll hear him. His impression of Elvis is excellent."

"We're here about vampires, not ghosts," Debbie said.

"Ghosts get more social media attention than vampires," Rolph said. "Everyone likes ghosts. Not everyone likes vampires."

"Room 202," I said. "My daughter will let you in right after Teatime. Why don't you guys get a cup and some scones while you wait?"

We pushed past them with Yena still in the bag and entered the utility room. I locked the door behind us.

"Please use some magic on her," I begged Missy.

She chanted a brief incantation, and the wolverines stopped struggling.

"Okay. How do we notify Lethia that we have her child—and do so in a way that we get maximum credit?"

"Why don't we lure her here and then stake her?"

"Missy! That's not like you! You're a nurse for vampires."

"The woman attacked your husband. Why do you care what she thinks of you?"

"She's our best—maybe our only—way to get to the Father of Lies and end all of this madness."

I reminded her of what I had learned in the Memory Archive about the Father of Lies falling in love with a mortal and bringing her back to life, albeit in a flawed way.

"His grand lie," I explained, "was that she would be alive and not actually an animated dead person."

"Let me get this straight: he loves her?"

"Yes. At least he once did."

"But instead of bringing her back to life as he promised, he made her a vampire?"

"Right."

"And she's not happy about it?"

"Nope."

"Plus, he steals her baby?"

"Yes. To save her the anguish of seeing the bestial thing she became."

"So why would she want anything to do with the Father of Lies?"

"Revenge," I said. "It's that simple."

"I realize she's a super-powerful vampire, but how can she harm him? He's a god, or demon—or whatever he is."

"I'm hoping she'll use his love for her against him. That maybe she can mislead the biggest liar of all."

"Your plan sounds far-fetched, I'm sorry to say."

"At the very least, I'm hoping she'll take her daughter and leave us alone."

"What if she's as horrified by the little monster as the Father of Lies thought she would be? As horrified as I am. She might be even more inclined to harm Cory and you."

She had a good point. I was totally winging it with my strategy, and it could backfire big time.

Stepping back from the problem, I remembered the sadness and loneliness Lethia was experiencing. It was enough for her to want to end her existence. And I remembered her nagging belief that her daughter wasn't dead and her desire to find her.

Even if her daughter was a feral fiend, reuniting with her would certainly have a profound effect on Lethia, right?

At the very least, she wouldn't be alone anymore. And maybe she would eventually tame her daughter.

A mother and her daughter should be together, even if they were blood-sucking monsters. Right?

I realized I might be under the influence of the complex dynamics between my own daughter and me. Perhaps vampires didn't look at motherhood the same way.

Yeah, maybe we should just use her daughter to lure her here and then stake her.

No, she's too powerful to stake. Unless Sophie rapidly improves her battle magic, setting a trap would not end well for us.

"I decided we need to go with the warm-hearted plan," I said.

"As opposed to the stake-in-the-heart plan?"

"Exactly. Lethia is too powerful for us to fight. We didn't go through all the trouble of rescuing Yena to get our butts kicked by her mother."

"I know vampires well," Missy said. "Some of them can be very affectionate. Lethia did not seem like the type."

"Mothers will be mothers." I felt bad reminding Missy that she'd never had a child. So, alas, she would never fully understand the bond. Especially between a mother and her daughter.

"Mom? Are you in there?" Sophie shouted outside the door.

"Yes, dear. This room is off limits to the other staff for a while."

"Why are you giving some social media influencer access to the Elvis ghost? We own the rights to that haunted room. We need him to sign a contract and pay us royalties."

"Okay, Sweetie. We don't have an intellectual property attorney, so you'll have to work that out yourself."

A task she can't conquer with an enchanted sword.

Sophie stomped off down the hall, and Missy and I were left to study Yena now that we had her out of her cave and in decent lighting.

She was pretty, like Lethia, with red hair that was longer than her height. Obviously, the Father of Lies hasn't been attending to her personal grooming. She growled from time to time, baring her fangs, but mostly looked like a sleeping toddler. I wouldn't say the pale, deadly fiend was adorable. But she was close to it.

I lifted her closed eyelids. Her eyes had the same rolling, unfocused quality as the vampires infected with the evil spell.

I mentioned the symptoms that were common between her and the infected vampires.

"From a strictly medical point of view, the similarity of the symptoms is important," Missy said.

"Could it be the same or a similar infection?"

"It's something we need to consider."

CHAPTER 23

VAMPIRE FAMILY REUNION

Not knowing where Lethia was, I had no way of sending her the message that we found Yena. My unreliable telepathy sometimes allowed me to send, as well as receive, thoughts. I put myself into a semi-trance in the Goddess's spirit and broadcast:

Lethia, we found your daughter.

I did this several times overnight. Who knows if she heard me? Yes, I was eager to reunite them, but I also wanted to get Yena off our hands before the little fiend needed feeding.

In the end, it wasn't my telepathy that conveyed the message. It was Mr. Jubbles. Only a couple of hours before dawn, he stopped by. I was downstairs and intercepted him before he could cause a conflict with Roderick or freak Debbie out.

"I'm here to see my niece," he told me, acting prim and proper, wearing a sport coat he had left behind that I returned to him on his last visit. It was a little dirty, though, as if Mr. Jubbles had been sleeping in a grave.

"You're not going to bite her, are you?"

"No. I have much better control of my appetite now. I'm here to give her 'the talk.'"

"'The talk'?"

"Yes. About vampires, and about how my survival depends on her discretion. Debbie is rather headstrong—"

"I noticed."

"—and I'm afraid she'll try to tell the entire world about us. Now that I have adjusted to my new existence, I realize how precarious it is."

"Good idea. She's in room 201. Please knock. Don't just appear beside her bed."

"Of course. Our family has proper manners."

I waited downstairs while he had "the talk." Hopefully, I wouldn't have to worry about Debbie anymore.

The crash of furniture rattled the ceiling. Debbie's room was right above me. Muffled shouts followed, but no screams. So far.

Did I need to go up there and interrupt their proper manners?

The sound of breaking glass. Not good.

Silence followed. I strained to hear what was going on. I thought I heard talking, so I resisted the urge to go upstairs.

Eventually, Mr. Jubbles reappeared in the living room.

"All is well," he said.

I studied his face and lips, looking for spots of blood.

"Are you sure?"

"Yes. I convinced her of the importance of discretion."

"You didn't bite her, did you?"

"Of course not!"

"It sounded rough and tumble up there."

"Debbie wasn't happy at first, but she eventually came around."

"So, she will keep her silence?"

He nodded. "I probably won't be invited to her home for the holidays this year, but there is peace between us."

"Excellent. Now, I have a favor to ask of you. Please tell your maker that we found her daughter and would very, very, very much like to reunite them as soon as possible."

CORY WOKE UP AND CAME DOWNSTAIRS AGITATED.

"What's wrong?"

"I was haunted by dreams of the vampire. I feel that she's coming for me."

I've heard that victims of vampire attacks are held in a psychological vise grip by their predators.

"Lethia might stop by. But not for you."

Cory had been filled in on Yena. He was not happy to have a feral vampire imprisoned in our utility room, especially not Lethia's daughter.

"I hope this will all be over soon," I said.

We were joined in the living room by Roderick and Diego. The inn was becoming Vampire Central.

"Do you sense her?" Cory asked them.

They nodded.

"She's coming for her child," I said.

"What if she rejects her child and comes after me?" Cory asked.

"I will protect you," Diego said.

"And I will certainly assist him," added Roderick. "I mean, I will provide moral support."

Diego shook his head in disdain.

I didn't need to send a group text. Instinctively, Missy and

Sophie had awakened and come downstairs to join us in the living room.

"We have quite a party going," I said. "Maybe I need to whip up some refreshments. Shouldn't someone be guarding the utility room?"

"I was hoping Lethia will break into it and take her baby," Cory said. "No confrontation needed."

"It's not that simple. We need to convince her to assist us in our cause."

"All I ask is to stay alive," Cory said. "That's *my* cause."

The doorbell rang. It was kind of anticlimactic. I was expecting Lethia's appearance to be more dramatic or stealthier. Then again, this could be a guest who lost their key card.

I went to the front door, followed by the two vampires and my sword-wielding daughter. If it was guests who were at the door, they would be a little put off by their welcome.

There, on the other side of the glass, stood Lethia. I unlocked and opened the door.

Lethia glanced at Roderick. He nodded, giving her permission to enter.

"You have my daughter?" she asked me.

"Yes. You finally can have her back."

"I didn't think she had survived. How did you find her?"

"Long story. The short of it is, Aastacki, the Father of Lies, took her from you when he brought you back from death. Yena was not herself when she came back. She has a mental health disorder. So, the Father of Lies hid her from you to keep you from being upset with him."

Lethia's face darkened with rage. "He had no right!"

"I know. Yena should be with you. She will require lots of care."

"I have all the time in the world. Bring her to me, please."

"Follow me. We've had to keep her in captivity because she's a danger to herself and others."

I led the way to the utility room, trailed by the vampires, Missy, and my daughter. Cory remained in the living room. I couldn't blame him. Roderick stayed there, as well, allegedly to protect Cory.

We were keeping Yena in a locked linen closet near the washers and dryers. Missy had added a spell to keep the door from being busted down. She removed the spell.

Before I could unlock the door, it flew from its hinges and nearly hit me.

"Good spell you have there, Missy," I said.

The vampires adopted defensive postures. Sophie's sword glowed purple. The closet door opened slowly. Yena walked with toddler steps cautiously into the room.

Lethia stepped in front of her, arms outstretched.

"My little Yena!"

The feral little vampire cringed with fear. Then, she studied her mother curiously. Finally, she said a word in an ancient, pre-Gaelic language. She repeated it over and over, pointing to her mouth.

"It looks like the child is hungry," Diego said.

"I'll take care of her when we leave," Lethia said.

She tried to hug her daughter, but Yena retreated from her, back into the closet.

"She has been kept from you for so long, and she's so young," I said. "Give her time."

"Of course."

Lethia appeared to be hiding her emotions from us. That's okay.

"I was hoping you can reward us for finding Yena," I said.

Lethia turned to me. "And how would I do that?"

"Please stop your war against the guilds. Most immediately, please stop trying to kill my husband."

"Yes, of course. That sounds fair enough."

I had expected either a more whole-hearted agreement or an argument. I guess I'll take it to the next level.

"Since Aastacki stole your daughter from you, why would you remain loyal to him?"

"Who says I am? After all, I agreed to disobey his orders to attack you."

"Right. And we were hoping you'd help us in more ways. Many years ago, Aastacki created a powerful spell and locked it in a box to enchant whoever was unfortunate enough to open the box. That happened to be the vampires of San Marcos. It's how they all lost their minds and became easy prey for you."

"Yes?"

"Can you persuade Aastacki to break the spell? This magic might even be the cause of Yena's . . . problems. If he breaks the spell, maybe it will help her, too."

"How will I persuade him to grant me this wish if I disobey his orders to attack you?"

"Well, I guess you don't have to mention that you're disobeying him."

"The Father of Lies always knows when he's being misled."

Yena chose that moment to lose it. If you think a toddler having a meltdown is scary, just imagine one who's a vampire kept in a cave for thousands of years.

Yeah. It was that bad.

Eyes rolling and drool flying, the little monster launched herself from the closet and tackled Diego. She howled like a nightmare as she sat on Diego's chest and tried to rip his throat out.

My friend was in an awkward situation. It was embarrassing

for a grown adult to be dominated by a two-year-old, although her many years of existence gave her more power than her diminutive appearance suggested. However, he couldn't fight back hard enough without looking like he was abusing the child.

Watching the struggle on the floor, I worried that, no matter how hard he fought, Diego was going to get his throat torn out.

It wouldn't be right for Sophie to slay the child with her magic—especially in front of her mother. I couldn't help Diego because I wasn't strong enough and would be torn to pieces in an instant. And the Goddess's healing powers haven't worked very well with crazed vampires.

"Mom? Can you get control of your child?" I asked Lethia.

"She doesn't know me."

"Missy?" I said out of the side of my mouth.

"Time for a nap, little girl," Missy said.

Her sleep spell kicked in just in time before Yena's fangs reached Diego's throat.

"Yena, you're so naughty," Lethia said, picking up her sleeping child. "I'll get her away from you before she causes any more trouble."

"I know you're taking on a great burden," I said to her. "But hopefully, she'll get better under the loving care of her mother. Aren't you glad I didn't take your hope away?"

She looked at me, confused.

"Hope will help you get through this," I added.

She clearly didn't know what I was talking about.

I got a chill as it dawned on me that something had been off about Lethia ever since she arrived at the inn—subtle things that had bothered me, but not enough to get my full attention. Finally, now I realized the truth:

This person holding Yena was not Lethia.

It was the Father of Lies.

CHAPTER 24

THE POWER OF LIES

The fake Lethia stared into my eyes and looked surprised. She must have seen the realization hit me.

Aastacki knew I was onto him.

"You actually believed I would be fooled by Lethia into helping you?" he asked, still in Lethia's voice.

Her face sagged. It was as if her flesh was putty that was melting off. As her face fell away, the Father of Lies' true appearance was revealed:

A bare skull that was humanoid, but not quite human. The eye sockets were elongated, the top of the skull was pointed, and the lower jaw was enormous with fangs like a saber-tooth tiger. Glowing red light came from deep within the eye sockets.

My view of the real Father of Lies lasted for mere seconds. He quickly changed into an old man—the harmless, mild-mannered, bearded gentleman the demon used as his human persona.

He smiled with sarcasm. "Don't try to steal my child again.

He quickly carried Yena to the door to the alley. The locks clicked open on their own.

"I'll see you around," he said.

But he never made it out the door.

Lethia—the real one—charged inside from the alley.

"Give me my child!" she screamed.

So surprised was The Father of Lies, he couldn't stop Lethia from taking her child from his arms.

Look, I've seen Aastacki defeat the God of War. It was highly unlikely a vampire could take him down. However, she was supposedly the world's oldest—and thus most powerful —vampire.

And she had another advantage: she was a mother whose child was in peril.

Like they say, don't get between a grizzly bear and her cub. That was exactly what the Father of Lies was doing.

He lunged for Yena in Lethia's arms. And she dodged him so quickly my eyes couldn't record her movement.

When he turned to come at her again, she freed an arm and raked her nails across his old-man face.

The old man disappeared. In his place was an exaggerated shadow of him—as if a spotlight were on the floor shining up at him and creating a menacing silhouette of a demon on the walls and ceiling.

Lethia, with Yena on one arm, tried to make a run for the door, but it slammed shut. She reached for the doorknob and yanked her hand away as if electrocuted amid a shower of sparks.

She turned to face the looming shadow, her eyes darting for escape routes. The inner door to the inn was covered by the shadow. She went for it anyway, but sank to her knees, screaming in pain as if she'd been sun-scorched. Yena still slept on her arm.

While the rest of us cowered in the corners, hoping to stay

out of the fight, I attempted to summon the Goddess. I didn't feel the burning inside me that indicated growing power. Instead, I was filled with compassion and empathy.

Sophie, however, was not on the same page.

"I will avenge the defeat of Haarg!" she shouted, her sword shooting purple lightning at the Father of Lies' shadow.

Nothing happened. It was like, well, shooting a shadow.

"Give me the child." The male voice was deep and seemed to come from the floor beneath us.

"Listen, Aastacki, I know about your love for Lethia," I said. "You hid her child from her for all these years, but you must allow her to have Yena back. Since you love her, you must do this."

The voice boomed through the floor: "Silence, mortal, or I will kill you."

"I speak with the authority of the Goddess Danu."

"A minor deity compared to me."

"An older and greater deity than you, Father of Lies. Danu is the mother of the world. You are only a trickster and manipulator of humans. Allow Lethia, as a mother, to have her daughter."

"When she sees what her daughter is, she won't want her."

"Father of Lies, you can cure Yena of her mental affliction. Don't you realize it is the same malady that infected the vampires after the box was opened?"

He was silent. It was rather nerve-wracking with everyone trapped in the room with an angry demon, not knowing what horrible things he could do to us.

"I created the spell long ago. I placed it in the box, knowing an overly curious species would open it. When humans appeared on the earth, I realized they would be the perfect target for the spell. It would sow irrationality and discord among you. To keep you enslaved to me by making you constantly fight one another. It turns out the spell was never needed. Humans naturally distrust one another and fight constantly without the spell. I can manipulate you as I wish without needing magic to do so. The box was lost and forgotten until a faerie learned about it and requested it from me to use as a weapon against you, Daughter of Danu. I never anticipated that vampires would be the ones infected."

"The spell is cruel to vampires," Lethia said. "My daughter has the same infection?"

"The same symptoms," Missy chimed in. "If you can break the spell and heal the vampires, the same treatment might cure Yena, as well."

"Why should I do this?" asked the Father of Lies. "The vampires mean nothing to me."

"For Lethia," I said. "Who means everything to you."

At this moment, I needed my reverse-telepathy. With the empathy of the Goddess still strong within me, I sent these words to Lethia:

Tell him you've always loved him. Tell him that if he cures your child —and the other vampires—you will be his consort. You must lie to the Father of Lies to make your daughter well.

Lethia stared at me. Her expression was defiant at first, but it softened before my eyes.

"Aastacki," she said. "I have said cruel words to you after you brought me back from death, and my existence wasn't what I had hoped. But that was unfair of me. I am grateful you made me immortal and overjoyed to learn you made Yena immortal, too. Her affliction is not your fault, and I have confidence you can heal her. I know this because I know I love you and always have. Since the days when you first pursued me, when I didn't yet know you were a god. I was a lonely young mother who had lost her husband to war, and you made me feel desirable again. After I learned who you were, and all the power you had, you continued to treat me with passion and respect. I say this now: I love you and want to be with you."

The ancient myths have plenty of tales of gods having hanky-panky with mortals. I'd never realized they could truly love mortals until I saw Haarg infatuated with Sophie and read the memories in the Archives of the Father of Lies' love for Lethia when she was human.

"You must not lie to me," the Father of Lies said to Lethia. "I see right through all lies. No one else can as well as I."

If he had any traits like a human's, he would have difficulty seeing through lies that told him what he wants to hear—that assuage his wounded vanity.

The insecurity I had detected in the Father of Lies came from being rejected by Lethia. That was his weak spot.

"I tell you the truth, Aastacki," she said. "Now that I'm immortal and have the wisdom that comes from spending thousands of years upon the earth, I see how petty I behaved when you brought me back from death. Now, I am prepared to rule at the side of a deity like you. The one I have always loved."

"Do you speak with sincerity?" he asked. There was the slightest tone of vulnerability in his words.

"I speak the truth, my love."

Man, she was a talented actress. Or was she telling the truth?

The Father of Lies' distorted shadow disappeared from the wall and ceiling. We all waited in silence for what would come next.

"Where can I find an infected vampire?" the booming voice asked.

"There is a nest at 11 Cordoba Street," Diego said. "Every vampire in the house is infected."

"I will visit them. You all must remain here."

Silence followed. Lethia tried the door to the alley, holding her hand near the doorknob to see if it would hurt her like before. There were no sparks, but the door wouldn't open. The locks were frozen, and the door remained secure, even after she kicked it with her vampire strength.

Someone was knocking on the interior door.

"Are you guys okay in there?" asked Cory.

"We're okay, but we're in the middle of a complicated negotiation."

I tried this door. It, too, wouldn't open.

"Is the door locked on that side?"

"No," Cory replied. He rattled the door. "I don't know what's wrong."

"I guess we have to see this thing through before the Father of Lies lets us out."

"Him? Oh, boy."

"Yep. The good news is, Lethia is not going to kill you."

She gave me a dirty look for being presumptuous.

"I hope," I added.

The waiting was unbearable, especially since dawn was near. There were plenty of places in the cavern-like utility room for vampires to bed down while avoiding sunlight, but I had no desire to be here with them while they did it.

And to be honest, Sophie would be dangerously tempted to stake Lethia if the vampire went to sleep.

It didn't help that Yena's sleep spell wore off, and the toddler was in a foul mood. Lethia was aghast at the problem she now had to manage. The motherly affection I had seen when she first held her daughter had been replaced by horror as the little one growled, kicked, and clawed.

Lethia fed her, allowing her to bite into a vein in her mother's arm. That quieted Yena for a short while until she began fussing again. And I mean a fussing that was a threat to all of us confined in here.

Just as I was about to give up hope of getting out of here without being bitten by a feral toddler, Diego jumped to his feet.

"Do you feel that?" he asked. "No, of course you don't. You're humans. What about you, Lethia?"

"Yes, I sense a change in the vampire hive mind."

"I remember when the vampires were first infected and how hard things have been for our community after it spread. I feel as if the gloom and curse are gone. Did the Father of Lies break the spell and heal everyone?"

"I did," his voice boomed through the concrete floor.

The ordinary-looking, harmless old man appeared out of nowhere. He approached the alcove where Lethia sat on the floor restraining her child.

The old man crouched and placed his hand on Yena's head. He pressed firmly as the child squirmed and tried to bite his wrist.

"It's the same affliction as the others," he said, "but not caused by magic. The one in Yena is more intractable, most likely because she's been ill for millennia. It is resisting me."

Being presumptuous again, I ventured over to the alcove.

"You need help," I said. "The healing powers of the Goddess. They weren't strong enough on their own to cure the affliction, but they can augment the power you're using."

Despite my feelings of revulsion for him, I placed my hand atop his on Yena's head. The Goddess's compassion and healing powers warmed me as they rose from my solar plexus and traveled to my hand.

My fingers trembled as the Goddess's benevolent powers mixed with the Father of Lies' magic. My fingers now hurt, as if suffering frostbite. An icy chill ran up my arm and into my torso. Panic arose in me as I realized I could be compromised and become possessed by the Father of Lies.

I needed to pull my hand away, but the complicated mixture of the good and evil powers held my hand atop the demon's like a magnetic force.

Sophie sensed my distress and came over, but she didn't know what to do.

Yena abruptly stopped growling. Her eyelids fluttered open, and she smiled.

"Papa?" she asked.

"No, child," said the old man. "I'm only your caretaker. Now, finally, you will be with your mother."

We both withdrew our hands, and I moved away from the creepy old man who was the demon's manifestation.

Lethia hugged her child, showering her with kisses. Everyone in the room relaxed to the point that I could sense it.

"She's healed," Diego said. "All the vampires are healed."

"There is a price you must pay," the Father of Lies said. "The vampires of San Marcos will now be ruled by Lethia."

Now it was Diego's turn to growl.

"*Rule?*" he asked with anger.

"*Lead*," Lethia replied. "Because Pedro was destroyed, the Clan of the Eternal Night needs a new leader. As the oldest vampire here by far, it is not unreasonable for me to take that role."

"There are others who are next in line to succeed Pedro," Diego replied. "Including me."

"This is not negotiable. Aastacki had tasked me with destroying your guild and replacing it with my newly turned followers. I speak as his consort and promise that you will not be destroyed. You should show gratitude for that."

I wanted to see the Father of Lies' reaction, but the old man had disappeared. I guess he felt fine being represented by Lethia.

Diego's shoulders slumped in resignation.

"Perhaps we can negotiate," he said.

"No, we will not. Tomorrow night, we shall hold the first meeting of the guild since the infection first spread. You will help notify the others, I trust?"

"Yes. Our hive mind is already learning."

"Um, Lethia," I said. "Can you assure me you won't turn my husband now?"

She smiled, revealing her fangs. "I have no plans to. Now."

I guess that was about the best I could expect.

"Where will you live?" I asked.

"Pedro's house will do fine. I was going to move in there before, but I was bothered by trespassers. I don't need to worry about them now."

She carried her daughter to the alley door, which opened easily.

"Wait," I called to her. "Do you take back the request you made of Danu?"

"Yes. I have a daughter to care for. And a city to rule."

The two disappeared down the alley too quickly for me to tell which way they went.

"Will you be okay with this?" I asked Diego.

"For now. I will enjoy having my friends back and an end to all the violence. One advantage to Lethia leading the guild is that she will be forced to stop turning humans. We'll all be safer for that."

Indeed, we would. I had mixed feelings about Lethia ruling the vampires. She had attacked my husband, turned Mr. Jubbles, and caused death and destruction for humans and vampires alike. I hated her for it. However, my empathy—and that of the

Goddess—was stronger than my hatred. I was happy she no longer wanted to end her existence.

Most of all, I looked forward to life getting back to normal. Well, normal being a relative word when it comes to my life.

The big question I had—and it might not be answered soon —was if Lethia had successfully lied to the Father of Lies. Was she putting on an act of love to get her way, or was it real?

Perhaps she, herself, did not know.

CHAPTER 25

UGLY EAGLES

I woke up with an angel standing at the foot of our bed. A rather nice way to wake up, I'd say. If I believed curing the vampires and getting Lethia off our back would make my life normal again, I forgot an important fact: for me, fantastical stuff is normal.

Cory was in a deep sleep, snoring away beside me, while Raphael stood there in human form, looking all gorgeous and perfect next to the duvet that now seemed much too drab.

"Good morning," I whispered. "To what do I owe this pleasure?"

And it was a pleasure. In Raphael's human form, he did more than meet my expectation of what an angel should look like, other than the shimmering field of energy that they normally appear as. Raphael always was more beautiful than any artist could imagine.

"Creatures have slipped through the Veil into this world," he said. "Harpies."

"Great. Just great. More ancient Greek mythological monsters, as if a cyclops weren't enough."

"Daughter of Danu, with all due respect, I am not always available to monitor the Veil for trespassers. This will be your duty: to protect this world and its creatures from harmful intruders."

"I never signed up for this job."

"When Danu entered you, she decided your path. And must I remind you that the world depends upon you to mend the tear in the Veil?"

"It's not something I can easily forget. Especially since I'm flummoxed over how to fix it."

"If it were easy, someone else would have been given the task. We angels cannot do it, either. The Veil was created by God but damaged by forces unleashed by mortals."

"The Fae are the ones who actually tore it."

"That is why we cannot trust them alone to repair it. You, we trust. You are a healer."

I guess that was a compliment. It didn't make me feel any better, though.

"So," I said. "Where are the harpies?"

The angel smiled. "That is for you to discover. I only know that they entered this world very recently. Since the hole in the Veil is closest to your city, I suggest you begin your search here."

His stunning visage faded away, leaving me with a view of my jeans hanging on the back of a chair.

"Were you talking in your sleep?" Cory said, groggy. "Boy, I'm hungry. Can't wait for breakfast."

Which was his passive-aggressive hint that I was late in beginning cooking the buffet breakfast for my guests—which my family and staff always got the first taste of in the kitchen.

After I dressed, I searched the internet for news showing

Harpy activity. Nothing for now. The harpies could wait. Several hungry humans could not.

I have a small television in the inn's kitchen that plays the local news and the morning shows while I make breakfast. It's an old-school habit that my mother also had. I don't know what younger, tech-savvy moms do nowadays, but a good old TV on the counter is fine with me.

I had just finished putting the scrambled eggs into the chafing dish when a news story caught my ear.

At a local high-school football game the previous evening, a large raptor of some sort had swooped down and snatched a football that had just been kicked for a field goal. It looked as if the kick was good for a score, but the bird flew away with it right before the ball passed the goalposts.

The news anchors made a lot of stupid jokes, but I was mortified. They played a video from someone's phone that showed the ball theft. It was very shaky and poorly focused footage. But it was remarkable to see the perfect kick, sailing right on the money, until the raptor grabbed it.

The anchors kept referring to the bird as an "ugly eagle," and when they zoomed into the footage, it looked very strange. It was too blurry for others to realize this, but since I knew what I was looking at, I recognized a tiny human head on the bird.

I worried that there were other videos of it. And what would the harpies do next? Snatch a puppy? Or a baby from its stroller? This could be serious, but there was nothing I could do about it until after breakfast.

When Sophie showed up to help me, thirty minutes late for her shift, I briefed her on the problem.

"I guess I'll have to slay me some harpies," she said, relishing the thought.

"You enjoy slaying things?"

"Monsters and evil creatures, that's all. I'm not a psycho, Mom."

"I didn't say you were. But heaven knows where you got this warrior gene. Right now, I need you to slay this mess in the kitchen."

After breakfast, I resumed searching the news on the internet for Harpy sightings but found only the football incident.

Some people think all the information in the world can be accessed on your laptop or smartphone, but that's so far from the truth. Most of the world passes these people by because no one posted something about it online. Monster sightings tend to be in that category.

When my phone rang, and I saw it was Samson, my jaw clenched. I doubted he was calling just to chat.

"There have been some incidents I thought you should know about," he said. "You gave me the impression that you're now sort of a guardian against weird stuff like this."

"I'm supposed to monitor the hole in the Veil for creatures coming through from the Underworld."

"Right. Well, it seems there are these eagles—"

"They're not eagles. They're harpies."

"Aren't they from Greek mythology?"

"Yep. And they're here in San Marcos."

"Yes, they are indeed. We got a noise complaint from an old man complaining that his neighbor was mowing his lawn too early in the morning. An officer went out there and found the ride-on mower, with no driver, running through the flower garden of a home down the street. She turned off the machine and spoke to the neighbor who made the noise complaint. He said he saw a giant eagle take the man from the lawnmower and fly away with him. The neighbor was thrilled about it and

233

thought it was a police eagle or something. That would be cool if we had those."

"How are you going to explain the man's death?"

"Oh, he wasn't killed. The eagle—I mean, Harpy—dropped him in a golf course lake. Aside from the bite from the alligator in the lake, he'll be fine."

"I wonder if there's only one harpy." I mentioned the football incident, which was already going viral.

My answer came soon enough, via another call from Samson.

Apparently, there was a large pack of cyclists. Yeah, you know where this is going. The coastal road, A1A, is very popular for bicycling, because there are long stretches without intersections and traffic lights—just miles of smooth asphalt with the ocean sometimes in view.

Large, organized groups of enthusiasts in their French and Italian racing outfits riding expensive bikes often take over the road. The ones I've met constantly complain about rude, dangerous car drivers, and I agree that there are a lot of jerks in sports cars who are dangers to the cyclists.

They retaliate by straying outside of the bike lanes and basically blocking any car from passing them. And woe be it to any pedestrian who tries to cross the street. I've been almost mowed down by speeding folks in skintight Lycra shouting at me to get out of their way.

Well, I learned that there was an entire flock of harpies that made it through the Veil. And seven cyclists were plucked from their rides and dropped two miles out in the Atlantic. Fishermen rescued them.

"You and Sophie need to get rid of these harpies immediately," Samson warned me, "before someone dies or captures good video of them."

And if the harpies kept up the attacks, what Samson warned about would be inevitable.

I needed to figure out where to find the creatures before their next attack. A few copies of the local newspaper sat on a table in the foyer for guests. A small headline below the fold caught my eye.

"This is too good for a harpy to resist," I said aloud.

Today, a ground-breaking ceremony was scheduled for a new office building on the outskirts of the city. It was controversial because it was on environmentally sensitive land where, coincidentally, many birds nested.

The developer, mayor, and several dignitaries were expected to show up, wear hardhats, and pose with shovels spray-painted gold.

I would bet all my money the Harpies would show up, too. In front of a lot of cameras. The article said the event was scheduled for an hour from now.

"Sophie! We have an emergency mission. Bring your sword."

WE ARRIVED AT THE PIECE OF LAND, WHICH HAD ALREADY been bulldozed free of any trace of life, before anyone else. Some construction workers were near an office trailer in the distance, but the dignitaries and press hadn't shown up yet. Which was good, because Sophie's method of slaying monsters was as subtle as a fireworks display.

Now, the question was, would the harpies come early, so we could dispose of them without being seen? Or do we have to wait for them to be attracted to the easy targets?

We waited. No harpies showed up.

Soon, a media-relations team arrived and set up a step-and-repeat photo backdrop emblazoned with the developer's logo and the Seal of the City of San Marcos. A TV reporter and cameraman, as well as photographers for the local newspaper and the county business journal, joined them.

"Shouldn't you keep your sword out of view?" I asked Sophie.

She was holding it as if she were preparing to battle orcs. At my suggestion, she slipped it between her body and our car.

A black SUV pulled up. The mayor and his aides stepped out. Next, two vehicles arrived carrying a man whom I assumed was the developer and several of his flunkies.

The media-relations team finished setting up a podium and turned on the wireless microphone. The event was ready to begin.

Still, no harpies had arrived. Maybe they were busy hunting more cyclists. I scanned the sky. Every time I spotted birds, my stomach tensed. The birds, however, were simply birds.

The tapping of a finger on a microphone blasted out of the loudspeakers.

"Good afternoon, everyone," said a woman in a business suit. Behind her stood the mayor, developer, and other people who looked important. "Thank you for coming to the official ground-breaking of the Grasslands Office Park, bringing innovation and new jobs to the county."

A smattering of applause came from a small audience.

A high-pitched trill, that sounded like it was from an eagle or hawk, made me look up in the sky.

A giant eagle was swooping in right toward the podium. As it got closer, I could make out the head of an angry, ugly lady atop the feathered body.

Before I could say anything, it swung over the podium, grabbing the wireless microphone in its talons and nearly knocking over the woman at the podium. The eagle soared back into the sky.

Sophie pulled out her sword.

"No," I said. "It's too public."

"Naughty, naughty, naughty humans!" a voice croaked over the loudspeakers. The Harpy knew English.

Then I spotted the rest of the flock. At least a dozen giant birds in a V-formation were approaching like a squadron of bombers. Both Sophie and I gasped.

The Harpies would cause havoc and, possibly, death. But Sophie shooting them down with her purple lightning would be too much of a spectacle—captured by dozens of cameras. There had to be another way to stop the Harpies.

"Raphael!" I cried in my mind and then aloud. "We need a gateway now!"

A familiar shimmering disc appeared near Sophie and me.

"It's not for us. Take those harpies up there away from here."

The gateway rose into the sky between the crowd and the approaching flock. I don't think the people noticed it, because they were too focused on the giant bird flying away with the microphone.

The gateway rose higher and intercepted the flock. The Harpies flew right into the portal and disappeared from the sky.

I sighed with relief. Just then, the first harpy returned overhead. It dropped the microphone, which landed on the developer's head. A loud "bonk" came over the loudspeakers.

Crisis averted. Saved by an angel.

SOPHIE GRIPED ABOUT IT AS WE DROVE HOME.

"Why do they need us if the angels can just take the monsters away?"

Raphael appeared in my rearview mirror, sitting in the back seat. Man, was he cute.

"Angels can't pass through the Veil into the underworld. That's Satan's territory. We can try to take the monsters back in history to their era, but that could cause untold problems that might change the course of history. Otherwise, we must dump them in the In Between, where they don't belong. When they cross into this world, destroying them is the best option."

"I'm okay with not destroying the harpies," Sophie said. "They didn't kill anyone as far as I know."

"As far as you know," I emphasized.

"If you repair the Veil, we won't have to worry about that anymore," Raphael said.

"You once promised that you would send two individuals to help me—one human and one of another species."

"I did. The human shall be your daughter. She has become extraordinarily powerful in such a short time. So much so that we decided she would serve just fine as your soldier."

"*We* decided?"

"The angels in charge of the sector of the universe where the Veil is damaged."

"And who is the individual from another species?"

"I will tell you when we decide. It might be a faerie because the Fae tore open the weakened section of the Veil. Or it might be a species that is unfamiliar to you."

"As long as I can communicate with it—and it doesn't try to eat me—I'll be okay with it."

"So, Mom, you and me working as a team. That should be interesting."

"We work as a team quite well when serving breakfast every morning."

"I'm talking about fighting monsters and saving the world. That's a little more important than toast and orange juice."

"Don't forget my scones," I said. "They are extremely important."

"The fate of the world does not hinge upon your scones."

"Some of our guests may beg to differ."

I noticed Raphael had disappeared from the backseat. Our mother-daughter banter apparently wasn't good enough for him to stick around.

"Wouldn't it be funny if Grammers helped us, too?" Sophie asked. "Three generations of Chesswick paranormals saving the world."

"I don't find that funny at all."

"Why do moms and daughters have such a close bond, but get on each other's nerves so much?"

"I think we'll be asking ourselves that question too many times to count."

WHAT'S NEXT

Book Ten: *An Angel's Touch*

Even goddesses can't catch a break.

Ever since the Goddess awoke in me, she's been a pain in the butt. The powers she gave me came with too many responsibilities. And now I face the greatest challenge of all: repairing the rift in the Veil that allows monsters of legend to pass through into our world and wreak havoc.

And boy how they keep coming.

Everyone has been on my case about fixing the Veil. By everyone, I mean the few humans who know about the rift and worry about being eaten by the monsters. And the angels who watch over the world. They're concerned I haven't been fulfilling my potential as mother-earth goddess.

How much will I need to sacrifice to accomplish this task? What happens if I don't fulfill my potential? Will I get fired?

Will I still have time to run my inn and serve the Memory Guild? Even goddesses can't multitask as much as that.

I have the feeling things will never be the same. And neither will I.

The forces of Heaven and Hell collide in the final book of the "Memory Guild" series. (The sequel series, "Memory Guild's Daughter," is coming soon.)

Visit Amazon or wardparker.com to get *An Angel's Touch*.

Meet my new paranormal mysteries series, "Monsters of Jellyfish Beach," coming soon. It features Missy Mindle and many characters from the Freaky Florida series. You can describe them as more crazy than cozy! Discover more at Amazon or wardparker.com

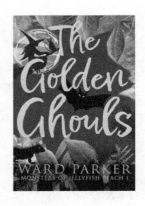

GET A FREE E-BOOK

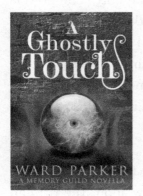

Sign up for my newsletter and get *A Ghostly Touch*, a Magic Guild novella, for free, offered exclusively to my newsletter subscribers. Darla reads the memories of a young woman, murdered in the 1890s, whose ghost begins haunting Darla, looking for justice. As a subscriber, you'll be the first to know about my new releases and lots of free book promotions. The newsletter is delivered only a couple of times a month. No spam at all, and you can unsubscribe at any time. Get your free book for all e-readers at wardparker.com

ACKNOWLEDGMENTS

I wish to thank my loyal readers, who give me a reason to write more every day. I'm especially grateful to Sharee Steinberg for all your editing and proofreading brilliance. And to my wife, Martha, thank you for your moral support, Beta reading, and awesome graphic design!

ABOUT THE AUTHOR

Ward is a Florida native and author of the Freaky Florida series, a romp through the Sunshine State with witches, vampires, werewolves, dragons, and other bizarre, mythical creatures such as #FloridaMan. His newest series is the Memory Guild midlife paranormal mysteries. He also pens the Zeke Adams Series of Florida-noir mysteries and The Teratologist Series of historical supernatural thrillers. Connect with him on social media: Twitter (@wardparker), Facebook (wardparkerauthor), BookBub, Goodreads, or wardparker.com

ALSO BY WARD PARKER

Freaky Florida humorous paranormal mysteries. Find them your favorite online retailers or at wardparker.com

The Zeke Adams Florida-noir mystery series. You can buy *Pariah* and *Fur* on Amazon or wardparker.com

The Teratologist series of historical paranormal thrillers. Buy the first novel on Amazon or wardparker.com

"Gods and Reptiles," a Lovecraftian short story. Buy it on Amazon or wardparker.com

"The Power Doctor," a historical witchcraft short story. Get it on Amazon or wardparker.com